# STAR WARS®

## THE CLONE WARS™

Defenders of the Republic

# STAR WARS

## THE CLONE WARS

**Defenders of the Republic**
adapted by Rob Valois

Grosset & Dunlap
An Imprint of Penguin Group (USA) Inc.
LucasBooks

GROSSET & DUNLAP
Published by the Penguin Group
Penguin Group (USA) Inc., 375 Hudson Street, New York, New York 10014, USA
Penguin Group (Canada), 90 Eglinton Avenue East, Suite 700,
Toronto, Ontario M4P 2Y3, Canada
(a division of Pearson Penguin Canada Inc.)
Penguin Books Ltd., 80 Strand, London WC2R 0RL, England
Penguin Group Ireland, 25 St. Stephen's Green, Dublin 2, Ireland
(a division of Penguin Books Ltd.)
Penguin Group (Australia), 250 Camberwell Road, Camberwell, Victoria 3124,
Australia (a division of Pearson Australia Group Pty. Ltd.)
Penguin Books India Pvt. Ltd., 11 Community Centre,
Panchsheel Park, New Delhi—110 017, India
Penguin Group (NZ), 67 Apollo Drive, Rosedale, North Shore 0632, New Zealand
(a division of Pearson New Zealand Ltd.)
Penguin Books (South Africa) (Pty.) Ltd., 24 Sturdee Avenue,
Rosebank, Johannesburg 2196, South Africa

Penguin Books Ltd., Registered Offices:
80 Strand, London WC2R 0RL, England

This book is published in partnership with LucasBooks, a division of Lucasfilm Ltd.

*Library of Congress Cataloging-in-Publication Data is available.*

ISBN 978-0-448-45464-1          10 9 8 7 6 5 4 3 2 1

# TABLE OF CONTENTS

# Clone Cadets

# CHAPTER ONE

*Fwooosh. Fwooosh.* The scream of blaster fire filled the air as explosions sounded all around. The enemy was closing in. A group of clone troopers known as Domino Squad cautiously made their way though the treacherous battlefield.

The clone troopers of the Grand Army of the Republic were the front line in the war against the Separatist Alliance, an evil faction led by the sinister Count Dooku, whose goal was to destroy the Republic and gain control over the galaxy. The clone army was created to defend the Republic from Dooku's massive droid army, a seemingly unstoppable force that had been wreaking havoc across the galaxy.

Suddenly, a massive army of deadly battle droids surrounded Domino Squad, blocking their way at every turn. The clones, easily outnumbered, returned fire, blasting away the best that they could.

Just then, their comlinks crackled to life. "This is command," a computerized voice announced. "You must break through enemy lines and take the tower."

Domino Squad immediately looked around for signs of the tower, knowing that it must be close by, but all they could see were waves upon waves of oncoming battle droids.

One of the clones called out over the clanking sound of approaching battle droids, "Comlink just relayed orders from—"

"We all heard the orders, Echo!" another clone interrupted as more blaster fire raced past their heads. His tone suggested that he was frustrated with the squad's lack of progress. Whatever their mission was, these clones were far from achieving it.

"Stop calling me that," the clone called Echo replied, obviously not pleased with his new nickname.

"Then stop repeating every order!" a third clone yelled from behind his protective helmet. All the clones were dressed in white clone body armor with similar green markings.

Clone troopers were identical, genetically modified soldiers created on the planet Kamino to serve in the Grand Army of the Republic. Created from the DNA of famed bounty hunter Jango Fett, they trained as soldiers from birth, and were regarded as one of the most efficient military forces in the galaxy.

These highly trained soldiers were identical in appearance, however they each possessed unique skills and personalities. Each clone was given a identification number, but over time most clone troopers adopted nicknames, often earned in battle.

Tearing through the smoke-filled battlefield, a clone brandishing a Z-6 rotary blaster cannon burst past Echo.

"Less yapping! More blasting!" the clone called to the others as he charged past. "Let's smoke these chrome domes and move onto the Citadel!" The six barrels of his mini-cannon fired blast after blast at the oncoming battle droids.

"CT-seven-eight-two!" Echo called out to the clone with the mini-cannon. "You're breaking formation."

But CT-782 kept moving, charging headfirst into the oncoming battle droids. "Just follow my lead, will ya?" he called back.

Echo sighed as the squad watched CT-782 quickly

mow down all the battle droids in his path. It was clear to Echo that this was not the way to complete the mission. Clone troopers were trained to follow orders. *There are rules for situations like these*, he thought, *and those rules need to be followed*.

"He's clearing a path," another clone, CT-28-631, said as he, too, broke formation and charged off after CT-782.

Echo watched as the clone broke all the rules and ran into the oncoming blaster fire. "I'm moving—" the clone added as he looked back at the others. But before he could finish his sentence, one of his fellow clones tackled him to the ground as droid blaster fire just missed his head.

"Thanks, CT-two-seven-five-five-five-five," CT-28-631 said as he pulled himself to his feet. He thought about his clone brother's name for a moment, and then said, "CT-two-seven-five-five-five-five . . . ?"

"It's Fives," the clone replied. "The name's Fives."

"Yeah, *five* pieces if you don't keep your head down," another clone, CT-4040, joked.

Echo looked first toward the oncoming battle droids, then back to his squad, who stood yelling and arguing in the middle of the battle. The Citadel was nowhere in sight. The team refused to follow orders from command or even stay in formation. Frustrated, he stepped up. "How 'bout we follow orders? This is our last practice test."

The other clones turned to face him. Even though they all wore helmets, he was sure he knew the looks on their faces.

"Will you shut up with the instructions?" CT-782 yelled. "You're not in charge."

No, Echo was not in charge. In fact, no one seemed to be in charge. As the clone troopers continued to argue, the battle droids advanced on their location.

High above the battle, the Togruta Jedi Master Shaak Ti watched from a secure observation deck. From this angle, the battlefield was revealed to be nothing more than a vast hangar-like training facility.

The clones themselves stood in the center of an oversized obstacle course constructed of raised and lowered platforms and with dozens of protective barriers positioned strategically throughout the floor. Four massive gun towers were erected in the corners, each with droids operating mounted blasters that fired down on the clones.

Below the observation deck, a multi-tiered tower rose from the floor. This was Domino Squad's final destination—the Citadel.

The battle currently unfolding was nothing more than a training exercise. Domino Squad, a team of young clone cadets, wearing simple practice armor, stood in the heart of an orchestrated battle. The battle droids were all being controlled from a computer in the observation deck.

# CHAPTER TWO

Jedi Master Shaak Ti stood on the observation deck with a solemn expression on her face. As a Togruta, her mighty blue and white montrals and lekku dominated her appearance. Her skin was a burnt red color, with distinctive white markings around her eyes.

On her face, she wore a prestigious Akul-tooth headdress, a sign that she had defeated a mighty Akul beast on her own. On her home world of Shili, the Akul was the only creature that the Togruta feared, and defeating one was a sign of strength.

As a member of the Jedi High Council, Shaak Ti was charged with overseeing the training of the clone cadets here on the planet Kamino. Her belief was that proper training was more important than experience, which made her perfect for this assignment. The clone army needed to be a flawless fighting machine, and any clone who could not pass her strict training would not be allowed to serve in the Republic Army.

Although the Jedi, as peace-keepers, had initially rejected the idea of the Republic utilizing an army of cloned soldiers, they soon realized that these soldiers were the Republic's only chance of defeating Count Dooku and his Separatist droid army. Now, not only had the Jedi entered the war, they had assumed a commanding role over the clone army.

Shaak Ti turned to face Bric and El-Les, the two bounty hunters who had been hired to help with the training of the clone cadets, and each carried the rank of Master Chief. "This particular unit seems to have some trouble," she said, referring to Domino Squad. "What do you recommend?"

Bric, a battle-worn Siniteen couldn't hide his disgust for the clones' performance. The Siniteen were a highly intelligent race with oversized, hairless heads that resembled giant brains. Bric's pupilless yellow eyes focused on Shaak Ti.

"Well, I'm no Jedi, so forgive my bluntness, but I say they fail," he said. "Send 'em down to maintenance with Ninety-nine and the other rejects."

The other bounty hunter quickly interjected. He was an Arcona and had dark, smooth reptilian skin and an angular head with large, yellow eyes.

"We can't fail them yet," El-Les responded. He seemed much more sympathetic to the plight of Domino Squad than his partner. "Remember, this is only a practice test. And, besides, the Citadel course was constructed to be a difficult challenge."

Bric was far from convinced.

The hyper-intelligent Siniteen were brilliant with numbers and details, and were capable of calculating complex hyperspace jumps without the use of a navi-computer. However they often viewed people in the same ordered fashion, and overlooked the possibility that they could change or adapt.

"Other squads we trained met the challenge, El-Les," he said. "Easily, in fact."

"Perhaps this squad is unique," El-Les replied.

"A clone's a clone," he said. "Nothing more, nothing less. Unique's got no place in war."

The Jedi interrupted. "Although I don't agree with his sentiment, Bric isn't wrong," she said as she turned back to watch Domino Squad struggle with their challenge. They were still nowhere near reaching the Citadel. "These cadets are far from perfect."

Back on the training room floor, the clone cadets continued to struggle.

"I can't hit anything from here," CT-782 yelled to no one in particular as he ran off and left the other clones behind.

"No, we have to follow orders," Echo turned and called after him, right before a blast hit him square in the chest and knocked him to the ground.

"The one they called 'Echo' never adapts to the situation," Shaak Ti commented to the bounty hunters.

Oblivious to his clone brother being knocked to the ground, CT-782 blasted away at a group of droids on a raised platform.

"CT-seven-eight-two seems to follow his own path," El-Les added. "He can't do it all alone."

Taking cover behind a barrier, CT-4040 and Fives argued about what to do next.

"You go," CT-4040 said. "I'll cover you."

"I'm a better shot," Fives replied. "You go."

"No, you go!" CT-4040 yelled back.

Distracted, the two clones didn't notice a team of battle droids coming up from behind. Seemingly from out of nowhere, blaster fire struck both of them, sending them both to the ground.

"Look at those two," Bric said, disgusted. "Argue on the battlefield, you end up dead." He looked down at CT-28-631. "Uh . . . and the last one."

Sure enough, CT-28-631 nearly got blasted as well. "I surrender! I surrender!" he called out to the battle droids.

"Need I say more?" Bric concluded.

Shaak Ti thoughtfully approached the computer that controlled the training exercise. "If these cadets can't get past their short-sighted selfishness," she said, "they will never come together. Unity wins wars, gentlemen."

She turned to the computer and spoke an order. "End exercise for Domino Squad."

As the computer began to shut down the exercise, Shaak Ti called to 99, a short, "defective" clone trooper who performed maintenance and cleanup work at the training facility. "Would you please send a cleaning crew to the training ground?"

"Yes, Mistress," 99 replied. "We'll take care of the mess."

Bric pointed toward 99. "You should tell that Ninety-nine to drag away the mess called Domino Squad," he said to El-Les as he exited the room.

Down below, Domino Squad regrouped.

"We almost had it this time," Echo said.

"Oh, yeah, and we all look nothing alike, either," CT-4040 joked.

CT-782 watched 99 come over and begin to clean up the destroyed bits of battle droids covering the floor. "Sorry about the mess," he said.

"Uh, it's okay, boys," 99 replied. "Nice try."

# CHAPTER THREE

Domino Squad stood silently as the lift lowered them from the floor of the obstacle course. As clones, they were not bred to accept failure.

Once outside the training area, Domino Squad made their way back to the barracks, stripped off their armor, and changed into their identical red cadet uniforms.

One by one, they passed 99, who was busy logging their weapons and helmets back into inventory.

"You know, you shouldn't worry," 99 said. "Most clones pass."

"Not all of us, right, shortie?" CT-782 replied with a gruff laugh.

99 ignored the insult and continued with his work. He'd never even been allowed to train as a

clone trooper. He had never been given a chance to prove that he could do more than clean up after everyone else.

As CT-782 continued to the locker area with the rest of the squad, he could hear the familiar sound of Echo complaining.

"C'mon, guys," he said. "We've got to follow orders."

CT-782 shook his head. How many times had he heard that before? *What good are orders and regulations when you have droids blasting at you,* he thought. *The battlefield has only one rule: The biggest blaster wins.*

"I don't know," CT-4040 added with a joking smile. "I think it went well out there."

Fives just glared at him and said, "Quit joking around." He agreed with Echo, mostly. They needed to follow orders to get through their training. If they failed, there would be no second chance. They would never become clone troopers.

CT-28-631, the clone who'd almost been shot in the head, stepped forward. "Can we stop arguing?" he asked.

CT-782 looked over.

"Can *you* stop being droid bait out there?" he

replied. From then on, CT-28-631 would be known as Droidbait. "You're getting in my way."

"Actually," Fives corrected, "*our* way."

CT-782 took a step toward Fives. "You want to be the best," he said, getting in the other clone's space, "you got to think like it. And I'm thinking like an ARC trooper."

ARC troopers were advanced clone soldiers—the best of the best.

"ARC troopers follow orders," Echo added, knowing what might happen.

CT-782 whipped around to face Echo. He moved in until they were face-to-face.

"Care to repeat that, *Echo*?" he barked.

Echo looked CT-782 in the eyes and said nothing. He just pushed past the other clone, bumping him hard as he did so. CT-782 spun around and tossed a fist at Echo. The two clones squared off, ready to finish things once and for all.

"Cut it out!" a voice yelled.

The clones all turned to see Bric standing there and immediately jumped to attention.

The Siniteen bounty hunter addressed the clones. "If you two would focus on fighting droids as much as you do on fighting with each other, you might stand a chance out there."

"Sorry, Master Chief," Echo said.

CT-782 was less apologetic. "Well, Master Chief," he said, "maybe our problems come from our training. I'd rather be taught by a Jedi than some mercenary bounty hunter."

"Jedi don't have the time to train grunts like you," the bounty hunter shot back. "That's why they hired me." Bric paused and looked the cadets up and down. "Listen, boys," he added, "when you were assigned to me I had high hopes for you. Now we're approaching the end of your training and you haven't advanced nearly enough. Even this bad batcher, Ninety-nine, has more sense than you guys do, and he's just a maintenance clone!"

Again, 99 tried to ignore the insult and continued to work, but he couldn't stop himself from turning to Bric and speaking for the other clones. "You . . ." he said, "you don't give them enough credit."

Disgusted, Bric turned to leave. "You're all just a waste of my time," he added as he walked away.

Domino Squad remained standing in silent anger.

Jedi Master Shaak Ti stood across from Lama Su in the Kaminoan prime minister's sparse, white office in the heart of the planet's capital, Tipoca City.

Like all of the cities on the water planet Kamino, Tipoca City was constructed as a network of domed buildings that were suspended above the ocean on mighty stilts.

The Kaminoans themselves were tall, thin beings with pale, white skin and long necks. Lama Su wore a sturdy, high collar that extended up the length of his neck and the ceremonial robes of his position.

Shaak Ti was worried about this most recent batch of clones, Domino Squad, in particular. Perhaps the Republic no longer had the resources to create fully functional clone troopers.

"I understand your concern, Master Jedi," Lama Su said. "Ever since the unfortunate death of Jango Fett, we've had to stretch his DNA to produce clones."

"A Jedi does not feel concern, Lama Su," Shaak Ti replied. "However, I've noticed this unit of clones has been . . ."

". . . Deficient?" The Kaminoan added. "My only recommendation is that you search the galaxy and find a suitable donor for your future clones."

The Kaminoans had developed and mastered this form of cloning technology generations earlier and had begun creating the first clones of Jango Fett well over ten years before the start of the Clone Wars.

They had been created in secret, even the Jedi High Council was unaware of their development. It was only after Jedi Master Obi-Wan Kenobi discovered the cloning facility on Kamino that the galaxy learned of the clones.

However, after Fett was killed by Jedi Master Mace Windu during the Battle of Geonosis, the clone army was put into use for the first time. Without Fett, there was no way for the Kaminoans to replenish their source of DNA.

Every time a new batch of clones was created, the DNA used was less and less pure. At some point, it would become unusable.

Another Kaminoan entered Lama Su's office carrying a tray of beverages.

"And what about the clones produced so far?" Shaak Ti asked.

"As you know . . ." Lama Su continued, "there is no one way to make a clone. Sometimes our efforts are less than successful."

"Are you suggesting we just cast off Domino Squad?" she asked. "They're living beings, not objects."

Lama Su paused for a second and then replied, "I thought a Jedi didn't show concern. Nevertheless, as general in charge of training, the decision on what to do with them would be yours, Jedi Master."

# CHAPTER FOUR

The next day, Domino Squad stood alongside several squads of clone cadets who were gathered on a hangar deck in the training area of the Kaminoan Military Complex, the largest clone training center on Kamino.

Bric stood ready to address the collected squads. Next to him was an ARC trooper in battle-worn armor marked with his battalion's insignia. The ARC troopers were some of the most skilled soldiers in the galaxy. Every clone trooper hoped to one day be among their ranks, but knew that only a rare few would.

"Gentlemen," Bric began. "Who wants to be an ARC trooper?"

"I do, sir!" the cadets called out, seemingly in unison.

"You have to pass your final test first," the Siniteen replied. "I want you to meet Commander Colt of the Rancor Battalion."

The ARC commander stepped forward. He was an imposing figure, full of confidence and experience. "I want you troopers to remember, we're shoulder to shoulder on those lines. Brothers," he said. "And sometimes we quarrel, but no matter what, we are united. Rule one: We fight together." He paused and scanned the young cadets. "So, who's ready to step up first?"

The ARC trooper looked around. "Let's start with the unit that ran the practice test in record time. ARC trooper time."

"Think he means us, boys?" CT-4040 said under his breath.

CT-782 tightened his face. He was tired of CT-4040's stupid jokes. He was tired of Domino Squad always failing. He wondered how he would ever become an ARC trooper if his squad couldn't even get it together long enough to graduate from training.

"Bravo Squad. Step up," Colt announced.

"Well, bravo for Bravo Squad," CT-4040 joked again, knowing that CT-782 hated it.

CT-782 could feel his fists beginning to clench, that should be him up there.

"Show an ARC trooper how it's done," Commander Colt ordered.

"Come on, boys," Echo whispered to his team. "Maybe we can learn something."

"Shut up, Echo," CT-782 growled. It was all he could do not to throw another punch at Echo.

From the observation deck, Commander Colt and El-Les watched as Bravo Squad maneuvered the Citadel obstacle course. Their actions were flawless. They moved as a unit, never once breaking from formation.

Time after time, Bravo Squad eliminated every droid and advanced to the next stage of the test. Every clone watched the others' backs—never arguing, never questioning orders. As a squad, they were perfect.

Colt nodded. He liked what he saw. "Impressive," he said. "You trained them well. Who's next?"

El-Les paused before responding. He knew that this wasn't going to go well. "Domino Squad," he reluctantly replied.

"How are they?" the trooper asked.

The Arcona paused again, not sure how to answer. Commander Colt looked at him curiously.

"We can do this, guys," CT-782 said as Domino Squad exited the lift and walked onto the Citadel obstacle course. They paused momentarily as they looked out on the scene of their previous failure.

"All we have to do is follow orders," Echo added.

As the clones prepared, they could here the members of Bravo Squad mocking them. "Check it out, guys," one of the clones said, "time to watch the dominos fall."

CT-782 grumbled softly as he tried to shake off the insult. He looked up to the observation deck.

"Begin the program," Commander Colt said, looking back down. "Let's not take it easy on them."

"All right," Fives said as he drew his blaster and readied for the simulation to begin. "We've got it this time."

"Oh, we'll win," Echo turned to face the others and once again said, "if we follow our orders."

CT-782 growled. He planned on making it to the tower this time, even if he had to do it alone. This was his one chance to impress an ARC trooper and he was not going to fail. "Here's your first order," he yelled to the others. "Follow me!"

With that, CT-782 raised his rotary-blaster and charged into the battle. The other clones looked at one another. The test had just begun and they'd already broken formation.

With no other plan, they followed after CT-782 and began blasting away at any battle droid in their path.

"They're getting farther than normal," El-Les offered from the observation deck.

"Maybe so," Colt replied, "but they're sloppy."

Bric gave a slight chuckle. "This is nothing," he said. "Give them their next set of orders and watch chaos ensue. I'm telling you, these guys just aren't ready."

# CHAPTER FIVE

The new orders were sent down to Domino Squad, who were busy scrambling toward their destination.

"Our orders are to flank the towers in a V formation . . ." Echo called out.

CT-782 ignored Echo and the orders and continued to advance on his own—he was going to do things his way.

The rest of Domino Squad moved into formation the best that they could.

CT-4040 let out a laugh as he tried to remember what his position was.

"I flank left," Fives called out to him. "You flank right."

"Take it easy, I'm on your side," CT-4040 joked. "Get it, *your side*, eh?!"

Fives shoved past CT-4040, not finding his joke all that funny.

Colt shook his head. "Pretty unorthodox."

Meanwhile, CT-28-631 broke formation and once again began following CT-782 who had moved farther off on his own, blasting his way through any droids that got in his way.

"Droidbait!" Echo called out to CT-28-631. "Behind you!"

But Echo's warning came too late. Blaster fire from a droid struck Droidbait's shoulder, knocking him to the ground.

"Man down!" Echo screamed as he ran over and knelt down next to his squadmate. "Form a cover shield."

Echo looked to the other clones, who stood their ground. *Why aren't they following procedure?* He wondered. *Forming a cover shield is standard procedure for a man-down situation.*

"Forget him," CT-782 called back to the others. "I'm breaking for the Citadel! It's just ahead."

Echo watched as the rest of the squad turned to follow after CT-782. The end of the course was in sight, and they'd never been this close to finishing. It didn't matter, Echo was not going to break the rules and leave a man behind. That's not what clone troopers do.

"Hurry," Fives called as he ran past Echo and the injured Droidbait.

"Guys," Echo pleaded with the other clones, "I think he's hurt."

"Leave him," Fives yelled back. "C'mon!"

In the observation room, Bric and Commander Colt followed the clones' performance.

"They've abandoned that soldier," Bric said. "You know what that means?"

"It gives us no choice," Colt replied.

"We're going to pass this time!" CT-4040 announced. But then all the droids shut down and a red light flashed in the room. "Okay, so I spoke too soon," he added.

"That would be putting it mildly," Commander Colt announced. Domino Squad had failed again.

El-Les and Colt made their way down from the observation platform to the training room floor. It was clear to the bounty hunter that the clone commanders were disappointed in Domino Squad's performance.

The clones stood at attention as Colt listed off their failures

"You broke formation, disobeyed orders," he said, "and you left a man behind. You broke rule number one."

"I'm sorry, Domino Squad," El-Les added. "This is an automatic failure."

Echo knelt back down beside the injured clone. "Looks like Droidbait here separated his shoulder."

"Someone take him to the infirmary," El-Les ordered.

# CHAPTER SIX

The bounty hunters Bric and El-Les made their way from the floor of the obstacle course and through the maze of corridors that comprised the Military Complex.

"I told you this was going to happen," Bric said to his partner. "We've wasted enough time on those losers."

"Their failure is our failure," El-Les replied. "I've made a request to General Shaak Ti that Domino Squad be allowed to repeat the final test."

Bric shook his head and then looked firmly at El-Les. "Why do you care about them?" he asked.

El-Les returned Bric's stare. "Why don't you?"

"I care about getting paid," he replied.

"It's a shame the bounty hunter in you sees this as only a job," El-Les said.

"More like an impossible task," Bric added.

El-Les didn't entirely believe his partner's motives. There were other, more lucrative ways for a bounty hunter to earn a living in the galaxy. Bric must have had some pride in the clones that he had trained.

"These cadets will be the finest troopers we've trained," El-Les added. "I have faith in them."

"Faith?" Bric laughed. "You can't be serious."

"We should treat them as a special challenge, Bric," El-Les replied.

"We should treat them as failures," Bric countered. "Besides, I've already requested that they be moved to cleanup and maintenance. That's all they're good for."

"Then I guess the general has a decision to make," El-Les offered, finishing the conversation.

Shaak Ti stood alone on the observation deck. She was lost in meditation as she stared off at the clone cadets training below her. The future of the Republic was in their hands. These soldiers were the only thing preventing Count Dooku and his Separatist Alliance from conquering the galaxy.

The war had grown to the point where it was difficult for even the Jedi Order to keep the peace.

There were new threats every day and the Republic's resources were growing thin. If Jango Fett's DNA was no longer capable of producing successful clones, then they needed to act quickly to find a replacement.

The Jedi sensed two figures approaching, clone cadets. Beyond the powers of the Force, Togruta were able to use their hollow montrals to detect the movement of people and objects around them. Shaak Ti broke her concentration as Echo and Fives entered the room.

"General, may we have a word?" Echo asked.

The Jedi Master turned to face them. Even though the young clones were accustomed to being in the presence of the Togruta Jedi, there was something about her that made them a bit uncomfortable. They were taught about the Jedi and their powers, but it all seemed a bit unnatural—at least to a bunch of clones.

"You're here to discuss your squad, aren't you?" she sensed.

Fives was caught off guard. "How did you know?" he asked.

"Jedi, mate," Echo answered.

Shaak Ti gave them a knowing look. "One doesn't need to be a Jedi to see the frustration on your faces," she said.

It was true—both cadets were at the breaking point. The thought of failing was taking its toll on all of Domino Squad.

"General," Echo began, "we'd like to request a transfer. To another squad."

"Bravo Squad, perhaps," Fives suggested.

"For the Jedi," Shaak Ti responded, her voice calm and even, "the individual and the group are one and the same. Much like you clones."

Echo though about this. "Which is why Fives and I are looking out for each other," he said.

"As individuals," the Jedi replied. "But not as a group. You are where you need to be. Solve your problems as a whole, not as individuals."

Echo looked to Fives, who had a puzzled look on his face.

Shaak Ti rose from her seat. "I've decided to allow you and the rest of your squad to take the test again tomorrow. "

Echo and Fives shared a look, neither quite grasping the Jedi's advice, but happy for the second chance to prove themselves.

Later that night, CT-4040 made his way to one of the complex's many landing platforms. As usual, there was a heavy rainfall and the droplets of water crashed hard against the deck.

The rainfall on Kamino was relentless, leaving the whole planet covered in cold, gray water. Standing on the edge of the landing platform, alone, was Bric. He appeared to be lost in thought as the rain splashed against his face.

CT-4040 approached the bounty hunter from behind. "You wanted to see me, sir?" the cadet asked.

Bric stood with his back toward the clone. "Near as I can tell, you're the reason your squad's a failure."

CT-4040 stopped in his tracks. He was expecting some kind of pep talk from the bounty hunter, not a reprimand.

"Ah, well, I'll take that as a compliment," CT-4040 replied, testing the rough bounty hunter with a joke.

Bric whipped around to face CT-4040. "It's all a big joke to you, right?" he barked. "Like those little nicknames you and your clone brothers give one another."

CT-4040 stood his ground against the bounty hunter. "Oh, I could think of one for you," he offered with a defiant smile.

"Funny," Bric replied. "But I think it's all just a cover." He paused for a moment and locked eyes with the young clone. "You hate me, don't you?" he asked.

CT-4040's heart was racing, Perhaps he'd taken the jokes a bit too far. "Oh, no. No, no, no. How could I hate you for doing your job? You're just pushing me."

"No," Bric smiled as he stepped closer and shoved the cadet. "This is me pushing you."

CT-4040 held his ground. His eyes burned as he fought to control his temper. Striking the bounty hunter would be the end for him. There's no way the general would allow him to finish training after that.

"C'mon, *clone*," Bric barked. "Hit me. Hit me, you joker. Can't take anything seriously, can you?" Bric grinned and stepped forward, his fist clenched. "You're a real cutup, aren't you?" He swung his arm low and connected with the clone's gut.

CT-4040 let out a small grunt, his stare fixed on Bric. Then he gave the bounty hunter a sly smile and said, "Thank you, sir."

"For what?" Bric snapped back.

"Cutup," he said. "I like the sound of it."

The newly named Cutup continued to smile as the bounty hunter's rage grew.

"Out of my sight, cadet," Bric ordered. "One way or another, you'll be out of this army. Count on it."

Cutup obeyed the order and marched away from Bric, who remained standing in the rain.

# CHAPTER SEVEN

In the infirmary later that night, Droidbait rested on a gurney. The room was humming with sounds of medical equipment as a medical droid tended to the clone's wounded shoulder.

El-Les made his way through the maze of gurneys and bacta tanks until he found the injured Droidbait.

"Diagnosis?" he asked the medical droid.

The droid turned to face the bounty hunter. "Minimal damage," it replied.

El-Les nodded at the droid's response. "I'll take it from here," he said as he picked up a bandage.

Unfazed, the medical droid moved off to help other patients. El-Les began caring for the clone's wound.

Droidbait opened his eyes slightly. The clone was surprised to see the Arcona tending to him.

"Sir?" Droidbait asked as he realized what was happening. He tried to sit up, but was too weak to push past El-Les.

"Easy now, cadet," El-Les said. "You need your rest. Big day tomorrow."

"I heard," Droidbait said as he stared up at the ceiling and thought about retaking the test. He felt like he'd let his squad down. *It was his fault they had failed the last time,* he thought. *If he hadn't been hit, they could've passed.*

"Maybe I shouldn't take the test again," he added. "I'm a liability out there, nothing but droid bait."

"No," El-Les said as he continued to work on the clone's wound. "I think any soldier, no matter who they are, plays an integral part. You'll never know if you don't try."

Droidbait thought about this. *What is my role on the team,* he wondered, *other than droid bait? How can I help my brothers succeed?*

Darkness filled the training complex as the members of Domino Squad drifted off to sleep. The next morning would be the most important day of their lives. What happened then would decide whether they'd be sent off to defend the Republic or live out their days as maintenance clones, cleaning up after future squads of cadets.

Later that night, as the members of Domino Squad slept, CT-782 crept from his bunk and quietly made his way through the barracks. This would be his final journey through the training facility.

He had with him a bag containing not much more than a change of clothing, that was all he planned on taking with him.

He wasn't sure how he'd make it off of Kamino, but he knew that there was no longer anything for him here. Especially if he wasn't going to become a clone trooper in the Grand Army of the Republic.

He'd heard stories of other clones who'd gone off to start lives on other worlds in the Outer Rim or far out in Wild Space. Some had become farmers or even mercenaries. Perhaps he'd become a bounty hunter. He had the skills and training.

Before exiting the barracks, CT-782 stopped at the weapons locker and stared at his Z-6 rotary blaster cannon.

"Going somewhere?" a voice asked from the darkness.

CT-782 spun around and saw 99 coming toward

him. "Get out of here," he said to the maintenance clone.

"You're going AWOL, aren't you?" 99 asked, looking at the pack on CT-782's shoulder.

CT-782 started to walk away. "Go back to sleep, Ninety-nine. This doesn't concern you," he said.

But 99 blocked his path. "You can't do this to your squad," he said.

"My squad," CT-782 blurted out. "We're nothing but a 'bad batch.' Failures. Like you."

"How can I be a failure when I never even got my chance?" 99 asked. "A chance that *you're* throwing away."

CT-782 thought about what 99 was saying. It was true, he *was* throwing away his last chance to become a clone trooper. But what would happen if he went out there tomorrow? Did they even stand a chance? Or would it just be one more embarrassing failure? Could he face the general or Commander Colt if they failed?

"You're always trying to be the anchor, *Hevy*. To do it on your own," 99 added. "Well, maybe you should embrace the fact that you have a team. See, I never had that. But you need them and they need you. Why carry such a *heavy* burden on your own, when you have brothers at your side, *Hevy*?"

"Hevy?" CT-782 replied. "Stop calling me that! We're just numbers, Ninety-nine. Just numbers."

"Not to me," 99 offered. "To me, you always had a name."

# CHAPTER EIGHT

Early the next morning, the members of Domino Squad began gathering in the barracks. Slowly they began to gear up, savoring every step of the process. This could be the last time they'd ever put on their armor and feel the pride that goes along with wearing it.

It was getting closer to start time. Echo took a deep breath and began running through their various formations in his head. Droidbait adjusted his armor over his injured shoulder. It still hurt, but he wasn't going to let it get in the way. Cutup just sat and smiled at the whole situation.

Fives double-checked his blaster as he looked around the room. "Hey, where's CT-seven-eight-two?" Fives asked.

"Yeah, where's CT-seven-eight-two?" Echo

repeated, noticing CT-782's cannon still on the rack.

They all looked at one another. Reality had sunk in.

Whether they liked it or not, CT-782 was the driving force behind Domino Squad. Even Echo knew that they'd have difficulty completing the course without CT-782 leading the way.

"If he's not here, we'll fail," Cutup said, the smile falling from his face.

"Not today, brothers," a voice called out. "Today we pass."

They all turned to see CT-782 standing behind them. He grabbed his mini-cannon and raised it in front of him.

"One more thing," he added. "The name's Hevy."

Together, a confident Domino Squad rode the rising elevator to the Citadel Obstacle Course. The lift clanked to a stop. There was a brief silence before the simulation activated—a moment that seemed to last an eternity.

Fives readied his blaster as he took a final deep breath.

The computerized voice relayed their first round of orders. The squad paused and looked to Echo.

Echo returned the look. "Orders came in clear, mates," was all that he said. There was no need for him to repeat a word.

"Nothing to repeat, Echo?" Cutup asked.

"Not today," he replied.

Hevy turned to Droidbait. "How's that shoulder treating you?" he asked.

Droidbait moved his arm around and smiled. "I'll live," he replied.

Hevy smiled as he nodded in agreement.

"We all know what we have to do," Fives added.

"Then let's do this," Hevy announced. "Together."

Like an explosion, the battlefield came to life. Battle droids sprang into action around them as blaster fire filled the air. Suddenly, Domino Squad was at the center of a war zone. Battle droids blasted at them from all sides. Shots came at them from all four gun towers. This time, though, the group stayed together, never breaking formation.

Together they moved from barrier to barrier, blasting droids and dodging fire.

"That's it, boys," Hevy called out. "Stay together."

"Fives, on your left!" Cutup yelled.

Fives quickly turned to see a droid rushing for

him. He took aim and squeezed the trigger, blasting the droid to pieces.

"Thanks, Cutup," Fives called as the two rejoined the formation and moved forward.

"Not a problem, brother," Cutup returned.

On the observation deck, Shaak Ti and the two bounty hunters once again watched as Domino Squad maneuvered the obstacle course. The Togruta Jedi's solemn expression masked any emotion.

The Arconan El-Les, however, could not hide his pleasure in seeing Domino Squad's notable improvement. "Look," he said to his partner. "They seem to be working together."

"Still early," Bric added with a wry smile. "A lot can change."

Something in Bric's tone made El-Les suspicious. Shaak Ti, seemingly oblivious, kept her eyes on Domino Squad.

"Keep it up," Echo called to the others as he advanced forward and blasted the head off of a droid. "We're doing great."

In a perfect V formation, the members of Domino Squad maneuvered past throngs of battle droids that were positioned above them on raised platforms.

As they made their way through the advanced stages of the obstacle course, the clones became more confident.

"We've never made it this far," Cutup called out. "We might actually pass."

Hevy wasn't ready to celebrate just yet. "No so fast," he replied. "Still got the Citadel!"

And there it was. The Citadel. The squad looked up to see it towering in front of them. On top sat their objective: a red flag.

Together, they rushed to a safe area at its base. Blaster fire crashed down around them. It was time to begin their preparation for the final stage. They needed to climb that tower.

"All right, prep the ascension cables," Echo said. "Let's scale this thing."

The team removed their packs. Ascension cables were long wires with hooks on the end that could be fired from their DC-15 blasters. The clones could then use the cables to climb to any location.

Hevy was the first to get his pack off. "Wait a tick," he said, searching its contents. "Where are the cables?"

The rest of the clones began rifling through their

own gear. None of them had ascension cables.

"They're not in our packs!" Fives added.

They looked at one another in disbelief, the sense of failure coming over them again.

"Just when things seemed easy," Cutup said.

Echo looked up at the flag. "We can't scale the face without them," he said. "We'll fail the test if we can't finish."

# CHAPTER NINE

Noticing the trouble down below, El-Les turned to face Bric, he suspected that his partner was responsible. "What's going on?" he asked. "Where are their ascension cables?"

"Must have gotten lost." Bric smiled, claiming responsibility.

"What did you do?" El-Les asked.

"You had faith they'd be the best, right?" Bric replied. "Well, the best pass. No matter what."

Turning to Shaak Ti, El-Les pleaded, "General, you have to stop this. This is unfair to the cadets."

"Adversity in war is a constant, El-Les," the Jedi explained.

"But Bric has cheated!" El-Les added.

"The enemy won't play fair, either," Shaak Ti offered.

Frustrated, Domino Squad stood in the safe area at the base of the Citadel. Somehow, the top seemed even farther away. The wall was covered with battle droids and gun stations. Even with the ascension cables, it would have been difficult to get past all the oncoming fire.

"We've got no choice," Echo said, lowering his blaster. "We can't pass."

"This is it, huh?" Fives asked.

"Not exactly," Hevy said, pointing toward a platform of gun stations on the wall above them. "Those guns up there. We can use them as steps to the next level. Form a chain and use one another to scale this face."

"Use the guns? Are you crazy?" Echo asked. There was too much blaster fire coming from the gun stations, and no way they could get anywhere close to them.

"Trust me," Hevy replied. "I know weapons. And those can be taken out with this." He held out his mini-cannon. "Just need a clear shot."

"How?" Cutup asked.

No one had an answer.

"Me," Droidbait offered. "I'll draw their fire, you guys blast 'em."

Before they could stop him, Droidbait made a run for it. Sure enough, the droids manning the gun stations on either side of the wall began firing away. Droidbait dodged their blasts and fired back.

The rest of Domino Squad seized the opportunity. Hevy stepped forward and began blasting the gun station droids. Echo, Fives, and Cutup quickly made a human ladder. Together, all five members of Domino Squad made their way to the first level of the Citadel. With the gun towers out of commission, the rest was easy.

"Well, I'll be . . ." Bric said, genuinely surprised by Domino Squad's ability to adapt. "Creative little clones, aren't they?"

"No unit has shown such ingenuity," El-Les added.

They continued watching as Domino Squad made their way to the top of the Citadel and claimed their prize.

Shaak Ti listened to the sounds of cheering coming from the floor below. Today was not just a victory for Domino Squad; it was a victory for the whole Republic. The clone DNA was not defective. For now, the future of the clone army was certain.

*But for how long would the DNA hold out*, she wondered. *So much was riding on the contents of one single vial.*

She turned to face the bounty hunters. "Bric, your actions have brought out the best in these cadets," she said. "Looks like they were trained well. Perhaps the finest cadets I've seen."

# CHAPTER TEN

"Congratulations," El-Les said as he entered the barracks. The members of Domino Squad jumped to attention. They were each dressed in official clone trooper armor with graduation medals pinned to them.

Long gone was the simple training armor that they'd worn for so long. Today they stood as true clone troopers—ready to join their brothers who were fighting battles all across the galaxy.

Hevy smiled to himself, wondering what his first assignment would be—maybe Christophsis or even aboard a Jedi cruiser. It didn't really matter, as long as he was on the front lines—blasting droids and defending the Republic.

"Next stop, ARC trooper," Fives added as if reading Hevy's mind.

"How about we graduate first?" Cutup joked.

They all nodded in agreement. The future could bring anything, but today was certain. They had all earned this graduation.

As they made their way out of the barracks and to the graduation ceremony, Hevy lingered behind. There was something he needed to do. He looked around and saw 99 standing in the back.

Hevy approached his friend, the one who'd taught him the importance of being part of a team. 99 smiled as he approched.

"You were right, you know," Hevy said to a proud 99. "About everything."

99 nodded. "I heard you were quite the leader out there," he replied.

Hevy thought about this and then slowly shook his head. "No leaders. We're a team," he replied and then pointed to 99. "All of us."

99 was touched. He was happy to be included, but knew that it would be over soon. Domino Squad would move on and he would remain behind.

"The army's lucky to have a clone like you, Hevy," 99 added.

"Not as lucky as I am to have a brother like you," Hevy replied.

"This is good-bye, I guess," 99 said. "Hevy ships out and Ninety-nine stays here."

"Eh, we'll see each other again," Hevy said, removing his medal. "How else am I supposed to get this back from you?"

Hevy pinned his graduation medal onto 99. "You deserve it," he added. "You're one of us."

99 smiled at the sight of the medal he never had the chance to earn.

Out in the hangar deck, Domino Squad was surrounded by the other graduating units. They all stood proud, ready to serve.

Shaak Ti faced the troops—another graduating class of clone troopers about to be sent off to battle. She wondered how many soldiers it would take to win this war. She herself had seen many battles and knew firsthand the cost of war.

"Today is your graduation," she said. "From here, you all ship out to fight against the Separatists and restore peace to the Republic. Congratulations. You are no longer cadets. You are troopers. May the Force be with you."

Off to the side, Bric and El-Les watched. El-Les was clearly proud of these new troopers.

"They are going to be a really formidable fighting force in the future," he said.

"We'll see . . . ," Bric replied in typical fashion.

"Atten-tion!" Commander Colt ordered. "Helmets on."

Domino Squad raised their official clone trooper helmets and placed them over their faces. Now, they really were troopers in the Republic Army.

# Rookies

# CHAPTER ELEVEN

Deep in the Outer Rim region of the galaxy sat the remote Rishi moon, a small meaningless rock floating in a seemingly meaningless part of space.

A lone Republic outpost perched on the rim of one of the moon's many deep craters. There were many small listening posts scattered throughout the Outer Rim that relayed information back to the Republic's central command.

Outside the outpost, a solitary clone trooper stood sentry on the outpost's landing platform. The clone scanned the distant, crater-poked surface with his macrobinoculars.

As usual, the green tinted display screen showed that there was nothing out of the ordinary to see. A few neebray flew in the distance, but otherwise nothing. In fact, this clone sentry had never seen anything out of the ordinary on this stark and desolate lunar plain.

He raised his macrobinoculars and activated his comlink. "This is the deck officer checking in," he said. "There's nothing going on . . . as usual."

The inside of the outpost's control center was just as quiet as the outside. It was a modest-sized room filled with screens and scopes.

Around the consoles sat the former members of Domino Squad in the same shiny white armor they had graduated in.

Their helmets were off as they worked their stations. It wasn't the glamorous post they had expected after their graduation from the clone training facility on nearby Kamino. But at least they had graduated and become real clone troopers.

Echo happily clicked through updates on his datapad while watching a holographic Bettie-Bot VJ dance on top of one of the consoles.

The song faded to an end. "You're listening to the Grand Army of the Republic Broadcast, the voice of the Outer Rim," the Bettie-Bot said. "This next one goes out to the mudjumpers of the 224th, slugging it out on Mimban. Keep your heads down and your seals tight, boys."

Fives let out a small laugh as the music started back up. The closest thing he'd seen to combat after leaving Kamino was watching Cutup try to arm-wrestle Hevy.

"Ha! Yes!" Hevy yelled as he pinned Cutup's arm. "Who's next? Fives?"

"Ah, shouldn't you be watching your scope, Hevy?" Echo asked, proving that some habits were hard to break.

Hevy gave Echo a sly smile as he shook his head. He no longer seemed as irritated by his fellow clone's by-the-book nature.

"Yeah, let's have a look," he replied as he walked over to his station and casually glanced at the scope. "What do you know . . . all clear. Just like the last hundred times I looked at it."

Hevy still dreamed of becoming an ARC trooper. He wondered how he would ever make it happen with postings like this. Why didn't they get stationed someplace exciting, like Mimban or Teth?

"Personally, I like that it's so quiet out here," Echo offered. "I can catch up on the reg manuals."

"Echo," Hevy growled, "what is wrong with you? We should be out there on the front line, blasting droids."

"Aw, leave him alone," Cutup added. "You know they left him in his growth jar too long."

"Yeah," Hevy agreed as he and Cutup shared a laugh. "You may not realize it yet," Hevy went on, "but we've landed on the most boring post in the Outer Rim."

"And one of the most important," a voice called from behind him.

Hevy turned to find Clone Sergeant O'Niner standing behind him. Cutup scrambled to his feet and turned off the music.

"Attention," Echo called out. "Sergeant on deck!"

The rest of the troopers all jumped to their feet.

"At ease," Sergeant O'Niner ordered. "Even though you are all new here, I shouldn't have to remind you that this quadrant is the key to the Outer Rim. If the droids get past this station, they can surprise-attack the facilities where we were born on our home world of Kamino."

They all nodded. They knew what was at stake.

"There are some officers on the way," the sergeant continued. "So I want everything squared away for inspection. Understood?"

"Sir, yes, sir!" all the clones responded in unison.

Just then, an alarm sounded. Fives turned to his

scope. Several large objects were on a collision course with the Rishi moon.

"Sir, incoming meteor shower!" Fives called out.

"Raise the shield," the sergeant ordered as the clone troopers hurried to their stations.

"You wanted excitement, Hevy," Cutup said as he made his way back to his station.

"Right," Hevy mumbled as he moved to his scope. "Oooh. Meteor shower."

# CHAPTER TWELVE

Aboard the Jedi cruiser *Resolute*, Jedi Generals Anakin Skywalker and Obi-Wan Kenobi patrolled the galaxy. They were in search of General Grievous, commander of the Separatist droid army. The cybernetic General was half living being and half machine—and would stop at nothing to see the Jedi destroyed.

The Jedi were almost certain that Grievous was planning an attack on the Republic—but they did not know where, when, or how he would strike. For weeks, Grievous had been eluding them. He was a master of strategy. He could attack from anywhere.

Obi-Wan entered the war room of the *Resolute* and found Anakin leaning on the holo-table, staring at a holographic map of the galaxy. His astromech droid, R2-D2, was beside him as always.

"Still here, Anakin?" Obi-Wan asked. "When was the last time you slept?"

Anakin had not slept much since they began the search for Grievous, and Obi-Wan was concerned for his former student. The two had known each other since Anakin was a child, and Obi-Wan couldn't help but worry about him. Of course, Anakin did make it easy for him to worry. Stubborn and impulsive, Anakin often let his emotions guide him. But there was no doubting his Force abilities. The Force was strong with him and he made an exceptional Jedi Knight—despite his unorthodox ways.

R2 let out a long, worried beep. He was concerned for Anakin, too. But the young Jedi was determined.

"I'll sleep after we find Grievous," a frustrated Anakin replied. "Clone intelligence spotted him in the Balmorra system, but that was weeks ago. Since then, he's vanished."

Obi-Wan rubbed his beard thoughtfully. "Well, unlike you, maybe he's getting some much-needed rest."

Admiral Wullf Yularen approached the Jedi. Like all admirals in the Republic Navy, Yularen was neither a Jedi nor a clone. "Excuse me, General," he said. "Incoming transmission from Commander Cody."

On the holo-table before them, a hologram of Commander Cody appeared.

"General Kenobi. General Skywalker," Cody addressed the two Jedi.

"Cody. How go the inspections?" asked Obi-Wan. Commander Cody and Captain Rex had been tasked with inspecting the Republic tracking stations to ensure that all were operating at peak efficiency. The Republic couldn't afford any weaknesses.

"The tracking station at Pastil is fully operational. Captain Rex and I are proceeding to the outpost in the Rishi system," reported Cody.

"Good," replied Obi-Wan. "Report back once you've arrived."

The mention of the Rishi system only made Anakin want to find Grievous that much quicker. The Rishi outpost was particularly important to the Republic's survival in this war, and with Grievous still on the loose, there was no telling what might happen.

Just south of the Rishi Maze lay the planet Kamino. It was there that the Republic produced the clones for its army. Hatched, grown, and trained at the planet's facilities, it was the closest thing the clones had to a home. If the droids somehow made it past that outpost, they could easily launch a surprise attack on Kamino and destroy the production of clones forever. The Republic army would be lost.

"Don't worry, Anakin," Obi-Wan said, seeing the Jedi's concern. "If General Grievous comes anywhere near this quadrant, we'll know about it."

Above the outpost, several dozen flaming meteorites tore across the sky and smashed into the outpost's shields, vaporizing instantly. However, a few managed to get past the barriers and slam down on the surface of the moon, creating giant craters in the ground.

On the landing platform, the clone sentry scanned the horizon with his macrobinoculars. In the distance he could see what looked like some kind of landing pod.

"What the . . . ," he said as he moved to activate his comlink.

But before he could report, a head rose into view. A commando droid.

The BX-Series commando droids were far more dangerous than the standard B1 battle droids.

Designed for stealth and infiltration, they were programmed with higher intelligence and designed for greater strength and speed.

A shock from a stun-baton to the back dropped the sentry to the ground. Several more commando droids climbed out of the pod as the clone's limp body was dragged out of sight.

"Get these doors open," a commando droid with the distinctive marking of a droid captain ordered, a vibrosword strapped to its back.

"Roger, roger," another droid replied as it tore open the outer control panel, its electronic voice much deeper and more threatening than its B1 cousins.

# CHAPTER THIRTEEN

"CT-Three-Two-Seven, report in," Sergeant O'Niner called into his comlink. "Sentry, do you copy?"

"Interference from the meteors?" Echo asked as he manned his control console.

From the outpost viewports, the clone troopers looked out at the landing platform for the sentry.

"I don't see him down there, Sarge," Fives called out as he turned away from the viewport.

O'Niner pointed at Droidbait and a trooper named NUB. "You two," he said. "Go find him."

The two clones grabbed their helmets and ran toward the blast door. As the door slid open, they saw six commando droids charging toward them from down the corridor, blasters drawn.

"Droids!" they yelled. This was the first time

that they'd seen real droids and they were caught off guard.

They turned to run back into the control center, but before they could make it back, the droid captain opened fire. The two clones dropped to the ground.

O'Niner threw on his helmet, grabbed his DC-15 blaster and charged down the corridor. Commando droids charged toward him, making their way over the lifeless bodies of Droidbait and NUB. "Sound the alarm," he yelled back and returned their blaster fire.

Hevy slapped the alarm button on the console. They needed to alert the fleet to send reinforcements. He waited for a moment, but nothing happened. He hit it again—still nothing. "They've disabled the beacon," he called back to the sergeant.

Fives, Cutup, and Echo put on their helmets and ran up behind him. Together, they stared at the twisted bodies of Droidbait and NUB. Their brothers, gone forever. They all knew that this was part of being a clone trooper, and even though they had trained for this moment, none of them were prepared for it.

"Get a message to the fleet!" O'Niner ordered, breaking their trance. "We have to warn—" A laser blast hit him in the leg before he could finish.

They all reacted with horror and surprise as their sergeant collapsed to the floor. On the ground, O'Niner struggled to roll over onto his back. He raised his blaster, but one of the commando droids kicked it from his hand. The droid looked down at O'Niner and fired its blaster straight at him.

"Sarge!" Hevy yelled.

The commando droids turned their attention to the remaining clones, who rushed back to the control room. Cutup hit a control panel mounted on the wall and the blast doors slammed shut. He popped open the panel and ripped out a handful of wires.

"That should slow those buckets down," he said as Echo opened a small hatch that led into a maintenance tunnel.

"This way! Hurry!" he said as a shower of sparks came from the blast doors. The droids were cutting their way through.

"No," Hevy protested as he finally put on his helmet.

"There's too many," Fives called as he crawled into the hatch.

Hevy looked back at the blast doors and saw the yellow sparks of the door being cut open. Making his decision, he followed the others into the hatch, closing it behind him.

By the time the commando droids had cut their way into the control room, the clones were gone.

# CHAPTER FOURTEEN

Just outside the Rishi system, a massive Separatist fleet prepared for invasion. There were dozens of well-armed Separatist frigates and giant Trade Federation battleships moving in formation. A swarm of vulture fighters maneuvered in and out of the larger ships. Once Grievous gave the word, they would advance onto their final destination.

General Grievous stood at the bridge of his command frigate. A hologram of the commando droid captain flickered on the console in front of him.

"The outpost is secure, General," reported the captain. "We shut down the alarm and turned on the all-clear signal," it continued.

"Excellent," said Grievous. "Keep that signal alive. I don't want the Republic to find out we're coming."

The hologram faded and Grievous paused for a moment to consider his imminent victory. With the Rishi outpost under his control, he knew that it would only be a matter of time until he would finally be able to destroy the clone-making facilities on Kamino. The Republic Army would finally be at his mercy. Not even the mighty Jedi would be able to stop him.

"Our spy on Kamino is making contact, General," called a droid from the communications console on the ship's bridge.

Grievous's eyes narrowed as he looked over his shoulder at a hologram of Asajj Ventress, one of the Separatist army's most ruthless assassins.

Even though she was one of Count Dooku's most trusted commanders, Grievous did not trust Ventress. She was trained in the dark side of the Force, making her feared throughout the galaxy—but she was wild, Grievous felt, like an animal. He was a true warrior, he would lead the Separatists to victory over the Jedi and the Republic.

"All the preparations for your invasion are in order," the assassin hissed. Her snakelike eyes peered out from under the hood of her cloak. The rest of her dark and sinister face was masked in its shadows.

"Good," responded Grievous. "Our fleet is approaching the system. We are almost at the rendezvous point."

"Very good," Ventress continued. "I will await your arrival."

"With the destruction of Kamino, I will stop their production of clones for good," Grievous laughed victoriously.

It seemed that nothing could stop him.

Grievous was unaware of the Republic attack shuttle *Obex* approaching the Rishi moon. The small ship broke through the atmosphere and headed toward the outpost.

Captain Rex sat at the ship's controls, piloting it toward the surface, while Commander Cody attempted to make contact with the outpost.

"Rishi outpost, this is Commander Cody. Do you copy? Rishi outpost, please respond."

There was no answer. Something wasn't right, perhaps solar flares had blocked transmission. He adjusted the comlink and tried again.

"Rishi outpost, come in! Rishi outpost, come in!" repeated Cody. He shot Rex a concerned look as he waited for a response.

"Sorry, Commander," a voice replied from the comlink.

Cody looked over at the console and saw the image of a clone trooper on the display.

"We're, um, experiencing technical difficulties," the trooper continued.

"This is the inspection team," Cody replied, more of an order than a statement.

"Inspection? Negative, negative. We, uh, we do not require inspection. Everything is fine here. Thank you," replied the clone trooper.

Cody looked to Rex who shared his concern.

"We'll be the judge of that. Prepare for our arrival," ordered Cody as he and Rex exchanged suspicious glances.

"Roger, roger," replied the clone.

Something wasn't right. *There is something familiar about that response*, thought Rex. He narrowed his eyes as he thought about where he had heard it before.

The clones made their way through the long, winding maintenance tunnel and into a drainage pipe that emptied out deep inside one of the moon's many craters.

"What do we do without the sarge?" Hevy asked as they kicked open the grill covering the pipe.

"Well," Echo replied as they climbed down the wall of the crater, "The reg manual says that the next—"

"Wait, wait," Hevy cut Echo off as a loud hissing sound filled the air. "Do you hear that?"

There was definitely a hissing sound coming from somewhere near by.

"Yeah," Fives asked. "What is that?"

"It doesn't sound like droids," Cutup answered.

"Don't forget about the giant eels," Hevy responded.

"I've never seen any . . . ," Cutup began to reply as a giant eel leaped from a cave-like hole in the crater wall. The massive creature grabbed Cutup with its mouth and lifted him off the ground.

"Cutup!" Heavy yelled as they opened fire on the eel. Their blaster fire bounced off of its skin as it dived back into another hole, taking Cutup with it.

Hevy fired his blaster pistol down into the hole, but it was no use. The eel was long gone.

"What was that?" Hevy asked.

"That was an eel," Echo replied. "And that's why we have the regulation not to go outside."

"Let's move before it comes back," Fives said as he waved the others along.

Echo paused before following. "Poor Cutup," he said.

As the clones made their way across the pitted landscape, they heard a familiar sound in the sky. Fives looked up and noticed a Republic *Nu*-class shuttle coming in for a landing. "It's the inspection team."

# CHAPTER FIFTEEN

The *Obex* hovered briefly above the landing platform before setting down. The ship's wings retracted into an upward position as it touched the ground. The ship's rear hatch opened and the clone officers exited the craft.

Outside the attack shuttle, on the landing platform of the outpost, Cody and Rex looked around suspiciously.

"This is not good," said Cody as they approached the outpost's blast doors. "I don't see the deck officer anywhere."

"These boys are sloppy," Rex added. "There should always be a deck officer on duty."

"I have a bad feeling about this," agreed Cody.

Something was definitely wrong. Suddenly, the blast doors opened and out walked a clone trooper.

"Welcome to Rishi, Commander," he said. His voice sounded like a clone, but his movements were oddly mechanical.

"As you can see, the outpost is operating at peak efficiency," he added. "Thank you for visiting and have a safe trip back."

Rex and Cody were not convinced.

"We need to inspect the base just the same," explained Cody.

As the clone officers continued toward the outpost, the clone trooper moved to block their path.

"We've got to warn them," Fives said from the crater. "Get on the comlink."

Echo activated the comlink built into his armor, but all he received was static. "It's no good. Their comlinks are on a different scramble set."

The landing platform was too far away. The clones could never make it there in time, even running at top speed.

"I'll signal them with this flare," Hevy said as he pulled a flare from his pack and loaded it into his blaster.

The three clones exchanged looks. This was their one chance to warn the others.

Back on the landing platform, Rex and Cody stood their ground in front of the clone trooper who was still trying to block their access to the outpost.

Rex stepped toward the clone trooper, he was done with playing games. "Take us to the sergeant in command," he ordered.

"Roger, roger," replied the clone. At the same time, the flare went off in the distance.

"A droid attack flare?!" Cody said as Rex instantly pulled his side arm and blasted the clone trooper in the face.

"Rex?!" Cody cried out. "What are you doing?"

"Relax," Rex said as he knelt down beside the remains of the clone and pulled off its helmet. "Just as I thought. Looks like one of those new commando droids."

Cody leaned in to examine the droid.

"That flare must have come from the survivors," he said.

All of a sudden, blaster fire came from the outpost, hitting the ground around them. Three commando droids appeared from the shadows and engaged the clones.

Cody fired a blast right at one of the droids, hitting it twice in the center of the chest plate. The droid collapsed to the ground, but immediately got back up and started blasting back.

"Those clankers have tough armor," Cody called out as he and Rex retreated toward the *Obex*. Two more commando droids appeared from near the shuttle, blasting away. The air was thick with blaster fire from both sides. Rex and Cody ducked behind some supply crates and continued to fire back.

"We're cut off!" said Rex.

Two more commando droids emerged from the outpost and hurled several thermal detonators at them.

"Off the platform!" yelled Rex.

"Copy that," responded Cody as he heard the metallic sound of the grenades hitting the platform.

Just before the grenades exploded, Rex and Cody used their ascension cables to lower themselves from the landing platform to the crater below.

The grenade blast destroyed the *Obex* and allowed them to escape unnoticed.

"No sign of them," the droid commando captain reported as it searched the destruction on the landing platform. "They must have been pulverized. Resume defensive posts."

"Well, *this* sure complicates things," remarked Cody when they were safely at the base of the crater.

"No worse than that time on Tibrin, Commander," Rex replied as he surveyed their location.

"We had Jedi with us on Tibrin," Cody added. "They helped."

Rex raised his arm to quiet his commander. He heard something moving in the distance.

In unison, they raised their weapons at the sound of approaching footsteps.

"Hands above your heads!" Rex shouted at the three approaching clones. "Take your sun bonnets off!"

The clones stopped short and raised their hands.

"Sir . . . ?" Echo replied, confused and a little frightened.

"Take them off! *Now*!" ordered Rex.

The three clones removed their helmets to reveal the familiar faces of clone troopers. As Cody and Rex lowered their weapons, another Rishi eel burst from the ground. It spun its massive head around and thrust itself at them.

Rex spun around and squeezed off one precise shot into the creature's eye. The eel let out one final scream as its limp body crashed to the ground. Rex and Cody removed their helmets as they knelt down to examine the creature's remains.

"Nice shot," Hevy said, impressed by the clone officer.

"The name's Rex," he replied as he touched the eel's wound, covering his hand in the creature's blue blood. "But you will call me Captain, or Sir."

As he stood, Five, Echo, and Hevy snapped to attention. "Sir, yes, sir," they all said in unison.

"And I'm your new boss, Commander Cody," the senior clone added.

Fives stepped forward and identified himself. "My designation is trooper two-seven dash five-five-five-five, sir."

"We call him Fives," Hevy added. "I'm Hevy and this is Echo."

"Where's your sergeant?" asked Cody.

"Dead, sir. We're all that's left," replied Echo.

"Looks like we got ourselves a batch of shinies," Rex said, unimpressed, as he looked over at Cody.

"Shinies, sir?" Echo asked.

"That's right," Rex added. "Your armor . . . it's shiny and new. Just like you."

The rookies all looked down over their brand-new armor. Rex then pressed his blood-covered hand against the breastplate of Echo's armor, leaving a blue handprint behind.

Hevy spoke up, "Sir, my batchers and I are trained and ready. We'll take back our post. Shiny or not."

Rex let out a small smile. "There's hope for you yet, rookie."

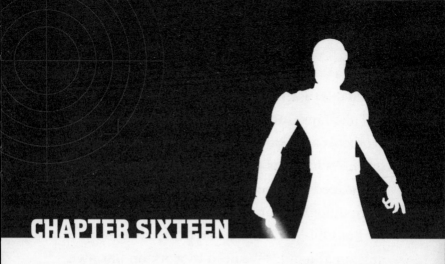

# CHAPTER SIXTEEN

Aboard the *Resolute*, Admiral Yularen stood at a communication station trying, without luck, to make contact with Cody and Rex. Obi-Wan and Anakin stood across from him, concerned that their clone officers hadn't reported in yet.

"Commander Cody, do you copy? Captain Rex, please respond," repeated the Admiral.

Although the two clones were supposed to have checked in once they'd reached the Rishi outpost, no one had heard from them.

"They should have checked in hours ago," Obi-Wan said. "It appears your captain follows orders as well as you do," he continued, with a sly look at Anakin.

Rex was Anakin's second-in-command, and like the Jedi general, he was freethinking and aggressive.

It was a combination that got them both in and out of trouble. They made an excellent team.

"Perhaps Cody is boring Rex with standard protocols and procedures," replied Anakin with a smile. As much as Rex had taken on Anakin's bullheaded behavior, Cody had adapted Obi-Wan's more thoughtful approach.

But Obi-Wan's mind had drifted back to the mission at hand. "We need to work on our own boring procedures and figure out a strategy to find Grievous," Obi-Wan reminded Anakin.

Anakin agreed. He would stop at nothing to defeat Grievous and bring the General's reign of terror to an end.

Back on the Rishi moon, the clones moved closer to the outpost. Echo, Fives, and Hevy followed behind Rex and Cody as they scaled up the side of the crater.

"Look sharp," Rex said as they made their way to the rim. "As long as those tweezers occupy this post, our home of Kamino is at risk." He then handed Echo his DC-15 blaster, retaining his two DC-17 side arms. Cody followed suit, and handed his blaster to Fives.

"But there's so many of them," Echo said as he cradled the blaster in his hands.

"Doesn't matter, kid," Rex said. "We have to retake this base, so we *will* retake this base."

Echo, Fives, and Hevy raised their blasters in acknowledgment.

"How do you propose that we get through those blast doors, Rex old boy?" Cody asked.

"I have a few ideas," Rex replied as he looked over at the outpost.

The other clones flanked the main blast doors as Rex approached, pretending to be a disguised commando droid.

"What was that?" a commando droid asked from inside the outpost as they heard Rex at the comlink.

The commando droids on guard inside examined Rex on the video display.

"Unit Twenty-six, is that you?" asked one of the commando droids.

"Roger, roger," responded Rex, trying to mimic a droid voice.

"You sound strange. Is their something wrong with your vocabulator?" asked the droid.

"Roger, roger," responded Rex again, in his best droid impersonation.

But the commando droids were still suspicious.

"Take off your helmet. Let me see your faceplate," the droid asked.

Rex stepped forward and out of the door's eyesight. While he was out of sight, he took a severed droid head and waved it in front of the door eye.

Watching from beside the door, Cody shook his head. "This is never going to work."

A moment later, the door slid open.

Rex and the others charged into the corridor and blasted at the commando droids. The group secured the area quickly and cautiously made their way toward the control center.

"Permission to take point, sir?" asked Hevy.

"*I'm* always first, kid," responded Rex.

Rex charged up the corridor. In the control room, three commando droids were monitoring different stations while a fourth stood in the doorway, his back to the clones.

He blasted the droid and the rest of the group stormed in, firing. The droids returned fire as they scrambled to take cover. Fives charged in from behind and took a blast to the shoulder, knocking him to the ground.

"Fives!" Echo screamed as he turned around.

"He's okay, focus on the battle," Cody ordered.

The commando droid captain fired at Rex, but Rex dodged the blast and fired back, shooting the droid's blaster out of his hand.

The droid tried again, lunging at Rex with his vibrosword, but Rex was too quick. He rolled out of the way, grabbed the droid captain by his head, snapped his neck, and slammed him to the ground.

Fives climbed back to his feet and moved in beside Cody as he moved farther into the command center. Hevy and Fives came around the other side and took aim at the last commando droid. They exchanged blasts until one finally hit.

"I got one," Echo called out.

"Sorry, Echo," Fives replied. "I junked that one."

"Sure you did," Echo called back as they went to regroup with the others.

As Rex examined the Captain, Cody noticed a tracking screen filled with tiny little blips. Someone was coming.

"Get to the window," he ordered. "Looks like we have more visitors."

They raced to the viewport. Echo lowered the macrobinoculars on his helmet and looked into the distance.

There, high above the outpost, he spotted what Cody saw on the monitor.

"It looks like a Separatist fleet," Echo confirmed as he saw two giant Trade Federation battleships surrounded by six heavily armed frigates.

"*That's* why they commandeered the outpost. They're mounting a full-scale invasion," concluded Cody.

"We have to warn command," added Rex.

# CHAPTER SEVENTEEN

Grievous stood at a command console aboard the
bridge of his command frigate as it moved through
the airspace above the Rishi moon.

*Why hadn't the commando droids reported in?*
he wondered.

"The Republic base is still transmitting the
all-clear signal," the battle droid captain reported.
"But for some reason our commando droids are not
responding."

Grievous was not pleased. This was meant to be
the easy part of his plan. A small group of clones
should have been no match for his commando droids.

"We can leave nothing to chance," he growled in
response. "That base cannot be allowed to alert the
Jedi that we're coming," he continued. "Send down
reinforcements to investigate!"

"Roger, roger," the droid captain replied, and ordered a landing ship to the outpost.

Back at the control center, Echo and Fives tried frantically to work the damaged communications console.

"Those clankers sabotaged our transmitter and hard-wired the all-clear signal," Echo reported as he examined the base controls. "It'll take time to repair."

"We don't have time," Rex replied from the viewport.

"Look!" Cody called as a Separatist landing ship entered the atmosphere.

"Well, buddy," Fives said to Hevy, "you always said that you wanted to be on the front lines."

Hevy watched as the Separatist ship touched down on the landing platform. Squads of B1 battle droids and super battle droids marched down the ramp and toward the outpost.

"We can't protect the outpost for long against that army of clankers," said Cody.

"Then we'll *destroy* the outpost instead," said Rex.

Five and Hevy exchanged a concerned look.

"But, sir," Echo called from the console, "our mission is to defend this facility at all costs."

"We have to warn the Republic about the invasion," Rex replied. "They'll take notice when the all-clear signal stops."

"That's right," Echo realized. "When they stop receiving our beacon, they'll get the message that something's wrong."

Rex thought about this for a moment, then said, "We'll need every thermal detonator in the inventory."

"It'll take more than a few detonators to destroy this outpost," Hevy offered.

"We can use the L.T.," Echo offered.

Rex and Cody looked at him.

"This moon freezes for over half the year," Echo added. "We use liquid Tibanna as fuel to heat the base."

"Liquid Tibanna," Cody agreed. "Highly explosive."

"Good. Bring the tanks here and prime the detonators," Rex ordered.

The battle droids marched their way closer to the outpost as Rex offered one more bit of encouragement. "All right, listen up," he said.

"There's only one target of interest in this sector: Kamino. It's the closest thing we clones have to a home. Today we fight for more than the Republic. Today we fight for all our brothers back home. Understood?"

"Sir, yes, sir!" Fives, Echo, and Hevy replied in unison.

As they put on their helmets, Cody nodded at Rex and then headed off with Five and Hevy. Meanwhile, Rex and Echo made their way to collect the tanks of liquid Tibanna.

"I think we can even the odds a little bit, Commander. Especially since they don't know we're here." Hevy said as they made their way into the armory. He went right for a Z-6 rotary blaster canon, his weapon of choice. "This one here is mine!" he said, raising the massive weapon in front of him.

Cody looked at Hevy. "A big gun doesn't make a big man," he said.

Outside, in the hallway, Rex and Echo escorted a plunk droid full of liquid Tibanna back to the command area.

Outside, the battle droids had reached the door. "Reinforcements reporting. Open up," said the battle droid sergeant into his comlink.

The doors hissed open and there stood Hevy, holding the cannon. "You didn't say *please*," he said as he opened fire.

The entire first droid squad was destroyed.

"Clones! Get 'em," another droid called as the squads charged toward the open blast doors.

The rest of the droids on the landing platform reacted quickly and advanced toward the blast doors.

Fives came alongside Hevy and tossed a thermal detonator in the fray. Its explosion knocked many of the droids off the side of the landing platform.

"We could use a Jedi about now," Cody said as he came around the other side and began blasting droids.

As the droids closed in, the clones retreated back inside the outpost, closing the blast door behind them.

In the war room of the *Resolute*, Admiral Yularen was still trying to reach Cody and Rex. Anakin and Obi-Wan remained beside him, anxious for word from the clone officers.

"Captain Rex, come in. Commander Cody, are

you there?" continued Yularen.

He turned to Obi-Wan. "General, there's still no response."

"What about the all-clear signal? Is the base still transmitting?" Obi-Wan asked.

"Yes, sir," responded Yularen.

"If something were wrong, they would contact us. We need to focus on finding Grievous," Obi-Wan replied.

# CHAPTER EIGHTEEN

Grievous paced frantically across the bridge of the frigate. This mission was taking much longer to complete than he had expected.

"What is the status of the base?" he screamed at the droid captain. "Is it secure?"

"Uh . . . ," the droid captain hesitated to reply. It had seen what Grievous did to droids when he wasn't pleased. "We've run into some difficulties . . . ," he continued. "There seem to be a few clones left, sir."

"Then wipe them out!" Grievous roared, almost knocking the droid from his chair. "We cannot let a few puny clones stop us."

Explosions rocked the blast doors open and the battle droids marched down the hallway toward the command station.

"Fall back to ops center," Cody yelled to Fives as he and Hevy held off the oncoming droids. The two clones continued to fire back at what seemed to be an endless tide of droids.

"Rex," Cody called into his comlink as he and Hevy backed down the hallway. "Time's wasting."

"Almost ready," a frustrated Rex answered from back in the command center. He and Echo were having difficulty connecting detonators to the liquid Tibanna.

"The handset isn't linking up with the detonator," Rex said to himself.

Rex tried the handset again. Nothing.

"Hevy," Rex called out. "This detonator isn't working."

"I'll take care of it," Hevy replied, taking the handset from Rex. "It'll be fixed in no time. I'll be right behind you."

Reluctantly, Rex left Hevy behind. "Just make it fast," he said. "Those droids are getting close."

Rex, Cody, Fives, and Echo ran into the maintenance hatch. Echo looked back at Hevy and left the hatch open for him.

"There, that should fix it," Hevy said as he reconfigured the detonator settings. He pressed the handset and once again the light flashed red. It still wouldn't link up. *This isn't good*, he thought. *There has to be another way.*

Hevy could hear the sound of droid footsteps approaching nearby. Quickly, he grabbed the mini-cannon and moved down the corridor, closing the hatch from the outside before finding a secure location.

He ducked behind a corner just as a squad of battle droids entered the command center.

"The base is ours again, sir," one of the droids said. "The clones are fleeing."

"Cowards," the command droid replied. "Secure the area."

Hevy cringed at the word *coward* as he clutched his blaster tight.

Out on the crater, the rest of the clones had grouped themselves behind a boulder some distance from the outpost, safely away from the impending explosion.

"Hevy, hit the . . . ," Rex called, and then turned to see if Hevy was with them. "Where's Hevy?"

"I'm on it, sir," came Hevy's voice over Rex's comlink.

"Hevy, get out of there!" Rex ordered.

But he couldn't let the droids win. His whole life he'd been trained to protect the Republic, but today he had something more important to do. Today he could save his home, Kamino. All his clone brothers needed him. *This is for them*, he thought. *For Droidbait and Cutup and all the other clones who gave their lives in service of the Republic.* He took a breath and activated his comlink. "The remote isn't working," he said. "I'll have to detonate it manually."

Just then, three battle droids entered the hallway and spotted Hevy.

"Hey, hold on there!" said one droid.

"It's a clone. Blast him!" said another.

They fired at Hevy. The others could hear everything over the comlink.

"Hevy!" Rex called. He needed their help. They would have to go back for him.

"Back to the maintenance pipe. Let's move!" ordered Cody.

"It's no use. I know what I have to do," Hevy said as he swung around with his mini-cannon and blasted away at the droids.

"I don't like your tone, rookie," Rex called back

as they made their way back to the pipe.

Hevy dropped to the floor, protecting himself behind his own blaster fire. He cut down the three droids and prepared to make a run for the detonator. Just then he was suddenly hit from behind. It was a jolt; Hevy had never been shot before. The blast whipped him around and he could see another squad of droids firing at him from the other end of the corridor.

He could hear Rex over his comlink. "Soldier, come in. Are you there?" And then a little more frantically, "Soldier, come in! Respond! Talk to us!"

Hevy was too distracted to respond. He lifted his mini-cannon and fired at the squad of droids as he backed his way into the control center.

The control center was overrun by droids. The battle droid commander was seated at the controls. Hevy aimed his mini-cannon and fired at the commander, destroying him along with several other droids that were standing nearby. But all of a sudden the cannon stopped firing. He was out of ammo. Lacking any other options, he threw the cannon at the droids, taking out a few of them. The remaining droids continued to advance on Hevy. He turned to dive for the detonator, but was hit several times in the back before he finally fell to the ground. Still determined, Hevy used his remaining strength to crawl toward the detonator. The droids stood over him, their blasters pointed.

"Do we take prisoners?" one droid asked another.

"I . . . don't," Hevy answered with his last breath as he pressed the button on the detonator.

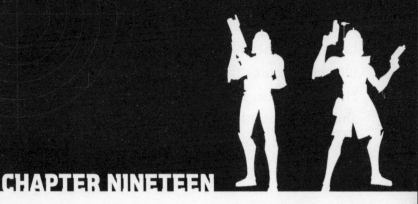

# CHAPTER NINETEEN

Cody, Rex, Echo, and Fives watched as the outpost went up in a tremendous explosion. The blast destroyed everything, including the Separatists' landing ship and all the surrounding droids.

There was nothing left except for smoking ruins. As much as they wanted to believe otherwise, there was no way that Hevy could have survived the blast.

None of the clones spoke for a while. Then Echo finally said, "Hevy always did hate that place."

Fives looked over to Echo and they shared an empty smile.

Echo couldn't believe that Hevy was gone. All through training he seemed so indestructible. Always happy to charge headstrong into whatever situation was put in front of him. And coming out unscathed every time. Echo had hated that about him.

The two clones were so different, it was hard to believe that they had come from the same DNA. But they had become friends. He had learned a lot from Hevy since their days on Kamino—how to be strong and how to be a leader. He would keep the best parts of Hevy with him always.

With the destruction of the Rishi outpost, the all-clear signal ceased to transmit. Aboard the *Resolute*, Admiral Yularen noticed that signal had stopped.

"The Rishi base has stopped transmitting!" the admiral called to the Jedi.

"It must be Grievous," grumbled Anakin.

"Sound the invasion alarm," Obi-Wan ordered to the crew. "Let's get this fleet under way."

The bridge crew sprang into action and within moments the fleet was on its way to the Rishi system.

From the viewing console on the Separatist frigate bridge, General Grievous's eyes squinted as he stared at the burning remains of the outpost in disbelief. He bellowed furiously and smashed his hands against the ship's controls.

"I didn't tell them to blow up the station!" he growled.

"Isn't it good that the base is destroyed?" asked the battle droid captain stupidly.

Grievous turned and glared at the droid captain. *Why were droids incapable of being anything but incompetent fools?*

"Idiot!" he said as calmly as he could. "The explosion will have destroyed the all-clear signal. Now the Republic will know we're here!"

As if on cue, the Republic fleet appeared in front of Grievous's viewport.

"The Republic fleet," he grumbled. "We're outgunned. Get us out of here."

From the surface of the moon, Echo watched the Separatist fleet retreat through his macrobinoculars. "We've got those tinnies on the run," he said.

"Thanks to Hevy," Fives added.

"Gunships," Rex called out as two Jedi gunships appeared overhead. Cody raised his blaster rifle in acknowledgment.

In the hangar bay of the *Resolute*, Echo and Fives stood in front of Obi-Wan and Anakin. Cody, Rex, and the other clone troopers flanked them on each side.

Echo and Fives stood at attention as the two Jedi approached them.

"On behalf of the Republic," Obi-Wan began, "we thank you for your valiant service . . . and we honor your comrades' sacrifice."

Not comrades, brothers. Echo and Fives looked briefly at each other. They were the only remaining members of Domino Squad, those five young clones who had become as close as brothers. They'd both heard that word many times, from General Shaak Ti, Commander Colt, and Captain Rex. But today they finally understood what it meant to be brothers. The memories of Droidbait, Cutup, and Hevy would be with them always.

"Your new unit is lucky to have you," Anakin added as he and Obi-Wan stepped forward to attach medals of commendation to Echo and Five's armor. "I would be proud to fight beside you. Anytime. Anywhere."

Obi-Wan and Anakin then bowed to Fives and Echo, who saluted in return.

After the Jedi left, Rex inspected the clones in their battered and dirty armor.

"Congratulations. You're not shinies anymore," he said.

"With all due respect, sir," Echo said. "We failed our mission. We don't deserve this honor."

"No," Cody replied. "If it weren't for you, the Republic wouldn't have learned of the Separatist invasion until it was too late."

"You showed me something today," Rex added. "You're exactly the kind of men I need in the 501st."

"Sir, yes, sir!" responded Fives and Echo in unison.

# ARC Troopers

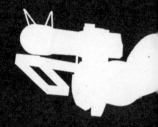

# CHAPTER TWENTY

Several months had passed since the destruction of the outpost on the Rishi moon.

Inside the war room of the Jedi cruiser *Resolute*, Anakin Skywalker and Obi-Wan Kenobi stood around an intercepted holographic message from General Grievous.

Flanking the two Jedi generals were Clone Commander Cody and Captain Rex. The message cut in and out, making it difficult to follow—but even through the broken and shaky images, it was clear that the message was between Grievous and Asajj Ventress.

A clone communications officer looked up from his console. "We're decrypting the audio, sir," he reported.

A moment later, the sound of Ventress's voice filled the war room.

"The planet of Kamino will be a dangerous target," she hissed.

Upon hearing "Kamino," Rex looked to Cody.

"Just make sure you hold up your half of the mission," Grievous replied. "We must stop the production of new clones if we are to win this war."

The hologram switched off and Anakin turned to face the others.

Grievous was planning another attack on Kamino, only months after his last attempt. Anakin felt that this intercepted message could be the key to stopping the General once and for all. With this information, the Republic could be ready and waiting for him.

Rex's face hardened. "They're going to attack our home planet," he said.

"The Separatists are taking quite the chance even considering this," Obi-Wan added.

"With all due respect, General," Rex continued, "if someone comes to our home, they better be carrying a big blaster."

"I concur with Captain Rex, Sir," Cody said. "This is personal for us clones."

Anakin stepped forward. "We'll make sure Kamino is secure. Tell your troopers in the 501st they're going home."

Rex nodded, he was ready to fight for his home.

Aboard the *Resolute*, Echo and Fives stood guard inside a cargo hold. Echo's battle-worn armor still had the blue handprint that Rex had placed on it back on Rishi—and both troopers now wore the distinctive blue markings of the 501st.

Since being reassigned, they'd been stationed on the *Resolute*, the flagship of General Skywalker and the 501st. In their short time with this new unit, they'd been across the galaxy and seen plenty of battles.

And while the 501st was a much more exciting posting than the outpost on Rishi moon, Echo and Fives were the junior men in the unit. That meant spending much of their downtime guarding supplies and taking inventory.

To fill up this time in the cargo hold, Fives had started telling jokes. It reminded him of their time back in the training facility on Kamino.

"C'mon, Echo," Fives added after delivering a punch line. "Don't you get it?"

Echo just stared back at him. "It was Cutup who was good at jokes," he replied. "Not you."

The two clones stood silently for a moment, remembering Cutup and their other lost brothers of Domino Squad. It seemed like a lifetime since they'd all been together back on Kamino.

"So what am I good at?" Fives finally asked.

"Obviously not unloading supplies from that gunship," a familiar voice said from behind them.

Fives and Echo turned to see Captain Rex heading their way. They quickly jumped to attention.

"As you were, troopers," Rex ordered. "Not too glamorous back here, but remember you're with the 501st. Best of the best."

"Yes, sir," Echo responded.

Rex looked to Fives, who remained silent. "Something on your mind, Fives?" he asked.

Fives took a moment before responding. "Sir . . . Echo and I," he started, "well, we've been with this unit through some rough campaigns, and—"

Rex interrupted. "You thought Commander Cody would've promoted you to ARC trooper by now."

Both Echo and Fives stood silently.

"You'll be ARC troopers when you don't have to ask for it," Rex said.

Rex turned to walk away, but paused to add, "One more thing, we're going home."

"Kamino . . . ," Fives said.

"It's been a long time since we've been home," Echo added.

"I'd hoped I'd return an ARC trooper," Fives said.

"We'll get our shot, Fives," Echo said. "We'll get our shot."

# CHAPTER TWENTY-ONE

Deep space. A massive Separatist *Dreadnaught*-class command ship tore through the void of nothingness.

On the bridge, General Grievous stood facing a hologram of a hooded Asajj Ventress, her pale, tattooed face barely visible.

"All is ready, General," the assassin reported.

"Good," Grievous replied. "We will attack Tipoca City first."

Tipoca City was the capital of Kamino and home to the Republic's main cloning facility—as well as the Military Complex where Domino Squad had trained.

"I have the exact locations of both the clone DNA room and the clone trooper barracks," she added.

Grievous laughed. "Both shall be annihilated under *my* hand," he replied.

"*Our* hands, General," Ventress hissed. "Count Dooku assigned us *both* to this task."

While both were high-ranking members of Count Dooku's Separatist Alliance, neither Ventress nor Grievous thought very highly of the other. Grievous thought himself an unrivaled military leader with no time for a savage assassin. And Ventress likened herself to Dooku and assumed that one day she would become his apprentice and eventually succeed him as head of the Alliance.

"But, of course, *assassin*," Grievous relented, knowing that he was the true leader of this mission. "I look forward to meeting you."

Ventress hesitated. "When can I expect your arrival?" she eventually asked.

"Soon" was all Grievous replied before ending the transmission.

Aboard her own ship, Ventress stood surrounded by a group of battle droids.

"Are the aqua droids prepared for phase two of the plan?" she asked.

"Roger, roger," the lead droid answered. Behind them sat a large bubble-shaped window, through which wasn't the blackness of space, but the deep, dark ocean—the ocean of Kamino. The Separatists had already arrived.

In the distance, teams of specially equipped underwater droids busied themselves assembling a fleet of menacing attack ships.

# CHAPTER TWENTY-TWO

Above the watery world of Kamino, a Republic shuttle raced through the gray, rain-filled sky and toward Tipoca City.

The shuttle touched down on one of the landing platforms that extended from the domed city. Moments later, Anakin and Obi-Wan exited the ship and quickly make their way over to Jedi Master Shaak Ti and the Kaminoan Prime Minister Lama Su.

Behind the two Jedi, Cody and Rex led the 501st, including Echo and Fives, from the shuttle. The clones looked around at their home. For many, including Echo and Fives, this was the first time they'd returned since completing their training.

"Masters Kenobi and Skywalker," Shaak Ti greeted her fellow Jedi. "Welcome to Kamino."

"Greetings, Generals," Lama Su added.

Anakin and Obi-Wan respectfully bowed to the prime minister.

Obi-Wan turned to face Lama Su, an obvious concern in the Jedi's expression. "I wish our arrival wasn't under such circumstances."

Shaak Ti gave Obi-Wan a worried look.

"We believe Grievous is planning a Separatist attack on Kamino," Obi-Wan continued.

"But the Republic blockade is far too strong," Lama Su said, looking to Shaak Ti. "They would not dare."

The clone troopers were led directly to the Military Complex. Rex and Cody needed to make sure that the facility was prepared for an attack.

Echo and Fives paused as they entered the main complex. This was the same building where they had spent their early years training and becoming clone troopers.

"Look around, Fives" Echo said. "Feels like yesterday we were here."

"Remember that?" Fives asked, gesturing to a group of clone cadets marching past in their simple training armor.

"Do I ever," Echo replied.

Then, in the distance, they heard a crash.

In unison they turned and saw 99 stocking equipment.

"Hey, Ninety-nine!" Echo called out.

99 looked up and immediately recognized them. "Echo! Fives!" he called back.

The maintenance clone put down the equipment he was stacking and walked over to Echo and Fives.

"You actually remember us?" Fives asked.

"I remember all my brothers," 99 replied as he looked around. "Is Hevy here?"

Echo and Fives stood silently for a moment, neither one willing to speak first.

"There was an incident on the Rishi moon outpost—," Fives began to explain, not knowing entirely what to say. The possibility of losing their lives was part of being a clone trooper, but it wasn't something they discussed.

"He saved our lives, but gave up his own," Echo cut him off, not wanting to relive the whole ordeal.

"Oh . . . ," 99 said solemnly. "I . . . I see." Then he pulled Hevy's graduation medal from his pocket.

Echo and Fives were surprised to see it, they never knew Hevy and 99 were so close.

"Hevy gave you his medal?" Echo asked.

99 could only nod. "So, why have you returned to Kamino?" he asked.

"The generals received word of an impending attack here," Echo replied.

Concern flashed across 99's face.

"What can I do to help?" 99 asked, clutching the medal in his hand.

# CHAPTER TWENTY-THREE

Above Kamino, General Grievous's fleet made their way toward the Republic blockade. Aboard his command ship, Grievous prepared his fleet for the confrontation.

"Attack formation Echo-3," he ordered.

His T-series tactical droid, TV-94, addressed the rest of the crew. "Status?" it asked in a tinny, mechanical voice.

The bridge battle droids offered updates, one by one.

"Deflector shields raised."

"Destroyers in position."

"Forward cannons ready."

Satisfied, TV-94 reported to Grievous that all ships were in position.

"Commence attack!" Grievous growled.

Admiral Yularen stood aboard the bridge of the *Resolute* and watched the approaching Separatist fleet: battleships, dreadnaughts, frigates, and destroyers all heading straight for the blockade. *A straight-on attack is an unusual approach for Grievous*, he thought. Something did not feel right.

"The fleet is pressing their attack, sir," a clone bridge officer alerted him.

"Contact command at Topica City," Yularen replied in his typically calm fashion.

The Admiral's report worried the Jedi. In the war room on Kamino, Obi-Wan pondered the oncoming attack. He, too, felt that this was an odd choice of tactics for Grievous. Why go for a straight-on assault when you can have the element of surprise?

Shaak Ti followed the advancing enemy fleet on a holographic display laid out in front of them. "The fleet is not as large as I expected," she commented. "Begin the air strike."

Obi-Wan closed his eyes briefly, hoping the Force would guide him in unraveling Grievous's plan. He could sense that things were not as they seemed, but he was unsure of what action to take.

Above the planet, the Republic held strong as blaster fire tore through space and collided with their ships.

Suddenly, Anakin's Jedi starfighter rocketed into formation along with a team of Y-wing fighters: Shadow Squadron. "Hope you don't mind a little company," he joked to his men as he took the lead position.

"Good to see you, General," a clone pilot named Broadside replied.

"You know me, Broadside," he added. "I'd rather be up here than stuck in a command center."

The fighters tore off and engaged the enemy fleet.

The battle raged on, the two sides exchanging blows. From Anakin's point of view it seemed that the Separatist fleet was taking a beating. Ships exploded around him as flaming pieces of wreckage made their way toward the atmosphere of Kamino.

"Warning! Falling debris!" a computerized voice filled the war room.

Shaak Ti looked to Obi-Wan. "Grievous appears to be sacrificing his transports in favor of protecting his command ship," she said.

Obi-Wan suspiciously eyed a hologram of a piece

of a Separatist ship falling toward the planet's surface. "Something's not right," he said. Once again he closed his eyes, he could feel the piece of debris making its way toward the waters of Kamino.

Back in the battle, Anakin led Shadow Squadron toward the heart of the battle. "Focus on the cruisers, Master," Anakin called over the comlink to Obi-Wan. "I'm going to press the attack."

Obi-Wan snapped back into the moment. The pieces were starting to come together.

"No, Anakin!" he ordered as he watched a hologram of the Separatist ships beginning to retreat. "It's too easy, not even Grievous would attack so recklessly."

"Master," Anakin replied, "the battle's up here in space, not down there."

Obi-Wan couldn't quite explain what he was feeling. "He knew we were ready for his attack," he explained to Anakin. "There has to be more to this than there seems." The Jedi paused in thought and then turned to Shaak Ti. "And those downed transports are the key. I'm certain of it."

"What are you thinking?" she asked.

Obi-Wan made his way toward the exit.

"Shaak Ti," he said, "I'd like to go for a swim."

The skies above Kamino glowed orange as enormous pieces of the destroyed Separatist ships plummeted from the sky and rained down on the planet. From the bridge of Ventress's underwater ship, she watched the pieces sink to the ocean floor.

"Reinforcements have arrived," a battle droid offered.

"Send out the aqua droids to assemble the assault craft," she ordered.

# CHAPTER TWENTY-FOUR

In the distance, Obi-Wan piloted a single-seater Kamino sub through the darkened water. The ship's small headlights offered him minimal light as he searched for wreckage of the Separatist ships.

All he could see was a group of Aiwha, giant flying creatures that lived under the waters of Kamino. These mighty beasts could use their wing-fins to propel themselves through water and even to soar through the skies.

*Majestic creatures*, Obi-Wan thought as he flicked on his comlink. "Nothing as of yet," he reported to Anakin.

"Only you could be worried about ships I already shot down," Anakin joked.

Obi-Wan smiled to himself. Then he spotted the wreckage.

As his sub got closer, he noticed something odd. It wasn't wreckage, but rather whole undamaged pieces of a bigger ship being assembled by a squadron of aqua droids.

The Separatist army had already arrived on Kamino. Grievous had deliberately allowed his ships to be destroyed so no one would think twice about all the debris falling to the surface of the planet. Debris that actually contained battle droids and pieces of attack ships that they were assembling on the ocean floor.

Grievous had allowed the Republic to intercept that message. The whole thing had been a trick and the Jedi had fallen for it. Obi-Wan had to warn Anakin, if they acted quickly it might not be too late to stop Grievous's invasion.

"Anakin," he called into the comlink. "I was right! Those downed transports were hiding ships for an underwater assault. Anakin, come in!"

There was no response. He waited and then tried again. Nothing. He'd have to return to Tipoca City to warn the others.

Obi-Wan grabbed the sub's controls and tried to return to the surface, but his route was blocked by a team of aqua droids, their blasters drawn.

"Hold it right there!" an aqua droid ordered. "Do not move!"

He smiled to himself as the aqua droids moved in closer to his sub speeder. He pressed a button on the ship's control panel and suddenly the sub exploded, pieces rocketing in all directions.

Obi-Wan was left with just a tiny, defenseless escape pod. With the aqua droids distracted, he directed the pod to the surface.

As the explosion settled, the droids spotted Obi-Wan escaping. They opened fire and blasted the escape pod apart. Obi-Wan remained calm, even though he was running low on oxygen and was too deep to make it to the surface. He had a plan. With the aqua droids closing in, he swam off in the direction that he came.

Above the surface, the rain was falling hard. Suddenly, an Aiwha broke through the surface with Obi-Wan on its back. As it reached the sky, it spread its wing-fins and glided the Jedi to safety.

Obi-Wan took a deep breath and patted the Aiwha on the back. "Thanks for the lift, friend." But his relief was short-lived. Separatist trident drills were attacking Tipoca City, tearing it apart. He pulled out his comlink. "Anakin, the city is under attack. I need you down here now."

"On my way," Anakin replied from the cockpit of his starfighter. He pulled the throttle hard and the ship rocketed toward the planet.

At that moment, Ventress's ship emerged from the ocean.

"The assault on Tipoca City has started, General," she reported to a hologram of Grievous. "You may begin your landing."

# CHAPTER TWENTY-FIVE

Anakin rushed into the war room on Kamino. Shaak Ti, Rex, and Cody stood surrounding a holographic display board of the city. The battle was unfolding in front of them as they tried to plan a way to prevent this assault.

"All right, everybody relax," the young Jedi announced. "I'm back."

Shaak Ti shot him a suspicious look. "Let's put that bravado of yours to good use," she said. "We can't let them breach the DNA room. That'll be their target."

"If they take out the DNA archive," Rex added, "no more clones."

"What about the cadets?" Cody asked, referring to the many younger cadets stationed at the cloning facility and training center.

"We'll take them to a secure location," Anakin replied. "No matter what, we fight."

"My thoughts exactly," Rex agreed.

As the city shook around them, Echo and Fives made their way to the hangar deck.

"Sir, you sent for us?" Echo asked an ARC trooper who looked to be in charge.

The trooper nodded as he surveyed the two clones. He could tell by their blue markings that they were members of the 501st. He knew that he could trust them with a difficult mission.

"It's dangerous, but I want the two of you up on the bridge in sniper positions," he ordered them.

"Yes, sir," Echo replied. "We're on it!"

Together, he and Fives raced off toward the bridge. Alarms buzzed and teams of clone troopers mobilized around them as they rushed into the battle.

This was the excitement they craved while standing guard on the *Resolute*.

As they exited the hangar, a trident drill ship ripped through the deck. Hundreds of battle droids spilled out of the ship, filling the hangar with blaster fire. Behind them, the powerful form of General Grievous appeared, stalking out of the ship.

"Kill them all," he barked to the droids.

Echo and Fives made their way down a corridor toward the bridge that connected the hangar to the cloning factories. Explosions rocked the city as they arrived at a secure position on the bridge. From this vantage point, they could see battle droids blasting their way into the factory.

Echo and Fives took their position and opened fire on the droids.

"Echo," Fives called out, "keep firing! We can beat these guys!" Then he spotted 99 coming up the bridge toward them.

"I brought some ammo," 99 yelled as he raced over, dodging blaster fire.

"Is there a better spot?" Fives asked. "A better defensive position we could take?"

Before 99 could answer, a squad of battle droids appeared behind them.

"Droids!" Echo called out. "Behind us."

Fives shoved 99 out of the way and returned the droid's fire.

99 wanted to do something. He had to find a way to help his brothers. Then he remembered something else in the bag of ammunition that he had brought.

"The grenades!" he yelled as he pointed to the

thermal detonators. Fives dashed to the bag and quickly tossed a grenade at the oncoming droids. *Kaboom*.

"Thanks, Ninety-nine," Echo said. "Good job."

99 couldn't help but feel proud. Then he saw more forms approaching through the smoke. "Look out," he yelled. "There's more!"

Echo and Fives raised their blasters, but as the smoke cleared, they saw the familiar shape of Anakin Skywalker charging toward them. Behind the Jedi a group of terrified clone cadets surveyed the destuction around them.

"General Skywalker," Fives called as he and Echo lowered their blasters. "Am I glad to see you."

"I'm looking for a secure location to take these cadets," he said.

"Sir," Echo offered, "the barracks'll be the safest place."

Fives and 99 nodded in agreement.

"I know the best way there," 99 offered.

"All right, Echo," Anakin said. "I'm putting you two in charge of these cadets."

Echo and Fives looked to 99, who was ready to lead the way.

"Clone-lings," Echo called out, "follow us!"

Echo nodded to Anakin and then he, Fives, and 99 led the young cadets off toward the barracks.

"Keep firing!" Grievous barked from amid the chaos. "No mercy!"

In the distance, groups of more advanced clone cadets concentrated their blaster fire on the trident drill.

Then, from behind them, a series of explosions rocked their location. The cadets crumbled to the ground as Asajj Ventress appeared from the destruction. She casually made her way over to Grievous. The two rival villains stood face-to-face for the first time, and, despite the battle that raged around them, it was as if they were alone.

"Your skills are impressive," Grievous began. "Perhaps a match for my own, assassin."

"Count Dooku may have taught you how to swing a lightsaber," she replied, "but it hardly makes you my equal."

"And yet I'm the general in charge of this assault," he growled. "Remember, assassin, you are here to recover the DNA."

"Why not just destroy it?" she asked.

"Because," Grievous replied, "the DNA could

unlock new possibilities for us."

Ventress made her way past Grievous. "Keep playing with your droids," she hissed. "I'll handle breaking into the DNA room."

Grievous reached out with one of his metal arms and grabbed the assassin by the wrist. "Shall I provide you with a droid escort?" he asked.

"My dear General," she shot back, "there's nothing you have that I could want."

# CHAPTER TWENTY-SIX

Inside the barracks, Echo, Fives, and 99 were surrounded by a large group of cadets and inexperienced clones.

A cadet stepped forward. "What are we going to do?" he asked.

Echo and Fives looked at each other. They were in command, but were unsure what to tell the others.

"A Separatist victory means death. For all of us," 99 added. "The cadet is right, what *are* we going to do?"

Echo and Fives exchanged another glance. Neither trooper had ever been in any situation like this before. Not even on the Rishi moon.

Rex's voice broke the silence. "We fight."

Everyone turned to see Rex and Cody enter.

"But our training's not finished," a cadet said.

Fives stepped forward, a determined look rising on his face. Captain Rex was right, just as he'd been at the Rishi outpost. The only path to victory was to stand up and defend what they held dear—whatever the cost.

"Look around," Fives said. "We're one and the same. Same heart. Same blood. Your training is in your blood. And my blood's boiling for a fight."

Echo stepped up next to him. Rex's words had lit a fire in him as well. "This is our home," he added. "This is our war."

Many of the young clones stood up. It was clear to Echo and Fives that they were ready to fight to defend their home.

Rex and Cody shared a look. They were impressed.

"What about weapons?" another cadet asked.

99 stepped forward. "The armory. It's just a few corridors away here in the barracks. I can retrieve all the firepower that we'll need." He looked to the clones and cadets. "So, who wants to blast some droids?"

Ventress skulked down the hallways of the clone facility. Her dark form was almost lost in the shadows. As she approached the door, she cautiously looked around.

Once she was confident that she had remained unseen, she flipped back her cloak and pulled out one of her lightsabers. With a flick of her wrist she ignited the blade and sliced a burning, orange hole in the door. The round piece of metal fell to the floor and she was in the room.

Inside the white, sterile room she saw a secure glass tube, which she knew contained the DNA of Jango Fett, the building block of all the clone troopers.

Ventress grabbed the tube and quickly exited the way that she'd come. Suddenly, she was violently hurled back into the room. Outside the door stood Anakin, his lightsaber ready.

"I was beginning to think my presence had gone unnoticed," she taunted as she leaped to her feet.

"You weren't planning on leaving without saying hello, were you?" Anakin asked.

Ventress ignited both of her twin, curved lightsabers and smiled a wicked grin.

Back inside the clone barracks, 99 confidently lead the clones through a maze of corridors and toward the armory. He knew this complex as well as anyone.

"Here it is," he said. "Everything we need is here."

"Excellent work, Ninety-nine," Rex replied.

"Hurry up," Cody ordered as he began to hand out blasters to the young clones. "The droids have almost reached the barracks."

The cadets held their blasters with both unease and pride. They knew that defending their home was the ultimate honor. This was what they had been bred for.

"Let's get into position," Rex yelled.

Out in the corridor, squads of battle droids made their way toward the barracks. Behind them, Grievous followed, confident in his victory. As they reached the final door, one of the droids stepped up, knocked, and said, "Open up."

Grievous roared at the droid's stupidity. "Get those doors open," he howled. "And scare every remaining clone out of hiding."

"Roger, roger," the droid replied and then ordered the others to blast the doors open. The doors eventually gave way, but instead of being met with a few cowering cadets, the droids were met by volleys of blaster fire.

The cadet army stood tall. This was their only chance to save their home.

"All too easy," Grievous laughed.

A familiar voice came from behind him. "Define easy, General."

Grievous whipped around to see a wet Obi-Wan standing behind him.

"Kenobi," Grievous growled as he ignited lightsabers in two of his robotic hands.

# CHAPTER TWENTY-SEVEN

Flashes of manic light filled the air as Obi-Wan and Grievous dueled. The cyborg's metallic arms moved with robotic precision, slicing and thrusting at Obi-Wan. The Jedi deftly blocked the oncoming assault as he held his own against the physically superior cyborg.

Grievous had defeated many Jedi in battle, claiming their lightsabers as prizes. Obi-Wan's lightsaber would be his greatest trophy. The two had battled before, and Grievous's only claim was that he'd never allowed the Jedi to capture him. For a warrior like Grievous, that was not a victory he savored.

The two opponents' lightsabers crackled with energy as they battled for control. Grievous's multiple lightsaber attacks pushed Obi-Wan back.

"Kenobi," Grievous taunted as he towered over the Jedi, "Kamino has fallen. Your clone army is doomed."

"I beg to differ, Grievous," Obi-Wan replied. He seized the advantage as he used the Force to send Grievous flying backward.

Grievous regained his footing and saw that the cadet army had advanced on his droids. He'd underestimated the Republic forces; this was not a battle that he could win.

Seizing the opportunity, Grievous fled. Obi-Wan charged off down the corridor after him. He couldn't let Grievous escape again.

As the battle raged around them, Echo and Fives held strong. Together, the remaining brothers of Domino Squad continued to blast away at the oncoming battle droids. The droid army's numbers were dwindling. It finally felt like they might make it through this.

"Cadets, now!" Rex ordered as the army of clones and cadets advanced forward with precision, as if they were full-fledged troopers.

99 followed behind Cody and Rex keeping them supplied with thermal detonators.

"Last one, Commander," Rex said as he handed Cody the grenade. "Make it count!"

Cody tossed the grenade, annihilating a phalanx of battle droids.

"I'll get more," 99 called out as he moved to head back to the armory.

"Ninety-nine, you can't," Rex called to him.

"I'm a soldier," 99 replied. "Like you. This is what I was bred for."

Just then, a voice came over Cody's comlink. It was General Shaak Ti. "The droids have been pushed back to the main hangar," she reported.

"That's giving it to the clankers," he replied.

99 charged past the clones and into the heart of battle. But he wasn't quick enough. Blaster fire hit him hard and he crumbled to the ground.

"Ninety-nine! No!" Echo screamed, but he knew that 99 wasn't going to make it.

Ventress spun her dual lightsabers as she charged at Anakin. The Jedi held his position, blocking the only exit from the DNA room.

She swung with two quick blows. Anakin dodged them as she deftly maneuvered past him and into the corridor. He spun and started chasing after her.

Meanwhile, Obi-Wan pursued General Grievous though the corridors, the massive cyborg using all his limbs to speed away.

Once out on the hangar deck, Obi-Wan paused. Grievous had vanished. Obi-Wan stood silently, trying to sense where Grievous might have gone.

Suddenly, from behind, the mighty cyborg lunged toward him.

Obi-Wan dropped to the ground and tumbled to avoid Grievous's attack. He leaped to his feet and raised his lightsaber in defense.

Just then, Grievous began to laugh. Seconds later, the ground shook and the landing platform teetered on its supports. A giant trident drill ripped through the structure, rocking the hangar back and forth.

Trying to maintain his balance, Obi-Wan took his eyes off of Grievous for a second. The general used this opportunity to make a run for one of the Kaminoan ships on the platform.

Obi-Wan darted after him, but it was too late. The platform's supports had given way and the Jedi was hurled over its side and back into the murky ocean of Kamino.

As he prepared to crash through the surface of the water, Obi-Wan took a final, deep breath. Debris from the collapsing landing platform crashed down in the water around him as he dived deeper.

Moments later, he found what he was looking for—his friend, the Aiwha. He grabbed onto the creature's back, who once again pulled him to safety.

"We've got to stop meeting like this, my friend" he said as they rose to the surface.

# CHAPTER TWENTY-EIGHT

In the hangar deck, Shaak Ti stood protectively in front of a group of ill-prepared clone cadets as a mighty octuptarra droid towered over them.

The clones blasted away at the giant spiderlike droid as the Jedi charged at it and leaped in the air. Deflecting its blaster fire with her lightsaber, Shaak Ti spun around and chopped one of its legs off.

The droid tumbled forward, allowing her to impale the droid's head with her lightsaber, destroying it.

Behind them, Ventress raced into the hangar. Anakin was only a few steps behind her.

"Look, it's General Skywalker," a trooper yelled.

"Move it, troopers," an ARC trooper ordered, directing their assault toward Ventress. "On the double. Fire!"

Ventress deflected and dodged their blasts as she looked for an escape route.

Anakin quickly dived forward and knocked the assassin to the floor of the hangar deck. The vial of DNA tumbled from her hands. She reached out to grab it but Anakin used the Force to pull it from her grip.

She flipped up and kicked some debris in the air. Using the distraction, she attempted to Force-pull the vial back. The small container of DNA sailed through the air toward her waiting hand.

She smiled at her victory, but it was short-lived. Before the vial landed in her hand, a clone dived forward and caught it.

"Arrggg," she growled as clone troopers surrounded her.

"I suppose you expect me to surrender?" she asked.

"Actually," Anakin stared at her, "I plan to let the clones execute you right now."

"Not this time!" She smiled as Grievous's ship swooped in overhead. A hatch opened on the Kaminoan ship as Ventress Force-pushed Anakin and the clones aside. She leaped up and into the safety of the ship.

Back in the barracks, Echo and Fives stood around the remains of the defeated droid army.

"We did it," a cadet called out. "We held them back."

They looked around at the cadets and could sense how proud they all felt because they themselves felt the same pride. They'd fought as brothers and protected their home. Then they saw Rex and Cody standing over the lifeless body of 99.

"We lost a true soldier today," Cody said.

"He really was one of us," Rex agreed.

Echo knelt down next to 99 and Fives stood behind him. The price of their victory, another fallen brother.

Echo and Fives stood on a balcony overlooking the vast gray ocean. Both troopers knew that this might be the last time they would ever see their home of Kamino.

"Echo, Fives," Rex called out from behind them.

The two clones turned and snapped to attention as Rex and Cody made their way toward them.

"You both really stepped up in the heat of battle," Cody said.

"We did what we had to do, sir," Echo replied.

"What any clone would have done," Fives added.

"Both of you showed valor out there, real courage," Rex said. "Reminded me of me, actually."

Echo and Fives shared a smile at this.

"Echo, Fives," Cody continued, "you're both officially being made ARC troopers."

"I don't think the Separatists will be coming back here anytime soon," Rex said. "But if they do, Kamino will be lucky to have clones like you defending it. Good job, men."

Stunned, they both stood in silence. It was a long road from the undisciplined clone cadets of Domino Squad to ARC troopers, but they both knew that this was where they belonged. For Droidbait, Cutup, Hevy, 99, and all their brothers, they would fight to defend the Republic at all costs.

# STAR WARS

## THE CLONE WARS

# Have you read them all?

## NOVELS

☐ **Bounty Hunter: Boba Fett**
978-0-448-45413-9 • $4.99

☐ **Decide Your Destiny:**
**#1 The Way of the Jedi**
978-0-448-45002-5 • $4.99

☐ **Decide Your Destiny:**
**#2 The Lost Legion**
978-0-448-45036-0 • $4.99

☐ **Decide Your Destiny:**
**#3 Tethan Battle Adventure**
978-0-448-45336-1 • $4.99

☐ **Defenders of the Republic**
978-0-448-45464-1 • $6.99
**New in October 2010**

☐ **Grievous Attacks!**
978-0-448-45003-2 • $6.99

☐ **Secret Missions #1:**
**Breakout Squad**
978-0-448-45035-3 • $6.99

☐ **Secret Missions #2:**
**The Curse of the Black**
**Hole Pirates**
978-0-448-45393-4 • $6.99

☐ **Star Wars: The Clone Wars**
978-0-448-44992-0 • $6.99

## GRAPHIC NOVELS

☐ **Ambush**
978-0-448-45039-1 • $7.99

☐ **The Battle for Ryloth**
978-0-448-45201-2 • $7.99

## FOR BEGINNING READERS

☐ **Bombad Jedi**
978-0-448-45038-4 • $3.99

☐ **Captured**
978-0-448-45202-9 • $3.99

☐ **The Holocron Heist**
978-0-448-45246-3 • $3.99

☐ **The Hunt for Grievous**
978-0-448-45394-1 • $3.99

☐ **Jar Jar's Big Day**
978-0-448-45223-4 • $4.99

☐ **The New Padawan**
978-0-448-44994-4 • $3.99

☐ **Operation: Huttlet**
978-0-448-44995-1 • $3.99

☐ **R2-D2's Adventure**
978-0-448-45222-7 • $4.99

## STORYBOOKS

☐ **The Battle Begins**
978-0-448-44991-3 • $16.99

☐ **Battle at Teth**
978-0-448-44993-7 • $3.99

☐ **Children of the Force**
978-0-448-45338-5 • $3.99

☐ **Meet Ahsoka Tano**
978-0-448-45034-6 • $3.99

## ACTIVITY BOOKS

☐ **The Dark Side**
978-0-448-45104-6 • $6.99

☐ **Intergalactic Adventure**
978-0-448-44997-5 • $4.99

☐ **Jedi Activity Cards**
978-0-448-45171-8 • $6.99

☐ **Sticker Storyteller**
978-0-448-45058-2 • $12.99

## MAD LIBS

☐ **Star Wars Mad Libs**
978-0-8431-3271-7 • $3.99

☐ **Star Wars: The Clone Wars**
**Mad Libs**
978-0-8431-3357-8 • $3.99

## MORE CLONE WARS FAVORITES

☐ **The Galactic Photobook**
978-0-448-44996-8 • $6.99

☐ **Heroes:**
**A Pop-up Storybook**
978-0-448-45203-6 • $24.99

☐ **The Official Episode Guide:**
**Season 1**
978-0-448-45247-0 • $12.99

☐ **Paper Model-Making Kit**
978-0-448-45004-9 • $19.99

☐ **Villains:**
**A Pop-up Storybook**
978-0-448-45463-4 • $24.99
**New in October 2010**